DEATH
of a
BUTTERFLY

Margaret Maron

BANTAM BOOKS
NEW YORK • TORONTO • LONDON • SYDNEY • AUCKLAND

This edition contains the complete text
of the original hardcover edition.
Not one word has been omitted.

DEATH OF A BUTTERFLY

A Bantam Crime Line Book / published by arrangement with the author

PRINTING HISTORY

Doubleday edition published 1984
Bantam edition / June 1991

*Crime Line and the portrayal of a boxed "cl" are trademarks of Bantam Books,
a division of Bantam Doubleday Dell Publishing Group, Inc.*

ISBN 0-553-29121-1

Published simultaneously in the United States and Canada

Bantam Books are published by Bantam Books, a division of Bantam Doubleday
Dell Publishing Group, Inc. Its trademark, consisting of the words "Bantam Books"
and the portrayal of a rooster, is Registered in U.S. Patent and Trademark Office
and in other countries. Marca Registrada. Bantam Books, 666 Fifth Avenue, New
York, New York 10103.

Printed in the United States of America

RAD   0 9 8 7 6 5 4 3 2 1

ICE QUEEN

It was too soon to know what Julie Redmond had been like in life, but in death she was still quite lovely. Her features were composed and drained of emotion as she lay on the polished kitchen tiles like a crumpled butterfly carelessly pinned for display.

"We haven't printed that yet, Lieutenant!" one of the lab men warned sharply.

Absentmindedly, she'd almost picked up the weapon, a heavy black flatiron. It was one of a pair that had been used as bookends for the short row of cookbooks now sliding in disarray on the wide windowsill. Sigrid doubted that the rough diamond-patterned handle would yield usable prints, but didn't press the point.

"If you wouldn't mind stepping back a little, Lieutenant?" suggested a photographer, his tone bordering on insubordination.

Sigrid turned and chilled him with such a frigid glance that he remembered that the privileges and power of rank extended to female officers, too, and abruptly decided to shoot another camera angle.

Having examined the body long enough to make her point, Sigrid moved past the lab crew, back down the short hall that led to the rest of apartment 3-D.

By Margaret Maron

For John—son and friend

CHAPTER 1

The peephole on the door of the service entrance to apartment 3-A was of the old-fashioned variety and offered a narrow perspective. Very little of the front door to apartment 3-D could be seen, just its outer frame. Easing the door open a hairline crack improved the watcher's hearing but further limited the field of vision.

The watcher, young and very determined, froze as the door to 3-D clicked open and a small boy emerged, clinging to the hand of a comfortably plump, grandmotherly woman.

"Tell Mommy goodbye, *caro*."

"Bye-bye, Mommy, bye-bye!" the child prattled happily. "Me besa good boy now! Bye-bye!"

The woman smiled at him indulgently. She was a well-tended sixty and her softly coiffed hair was jet black with just a light threading of gray. She wore frivolous black patent shoes that matched her purse and a stylish suit of floral silk that flattered her ample proportions and that also, thought the watching girl, had probably cost a full week's salary.

"—trouble?" the woman was asking. "When was Timmy any trouble to us? You take your time, Julie."

She closed the door and the child pulled her through the peephole's field of vision to the elevator.

"Want Mama Luisa to lift you up, *caro mio*?"

"I-me puncha button!" he gleefully agreed.

When they had departed, the landing was quiet for another half hour. Then a door out of view must have opened, for male voices were heard, but too indistinctly to catch the import until the elevator door swooshed open and an earnest voice said, "Thanks, Vico. It means a hell of a lot."

Through the thick walls by the elevator shaft, the girl could hear the cage come and go to other floors, but it was another ten minutes before the elevator again rose to a new summons from this landing and someone from 3-B descended on it.

She idly wondered who. Of the four apartments which opened onto this landing, only the traffic to and from 3-D, Julie Redmond's apartment, was important; yet any activity broke the monotony.

And how monotonous it was! Probably futile, too. Julie seemed to lead such a virtuous life these days that her suspicions were starting to seem absurd. If it weren't for that odd note she'd found under George's desk and his missing Saturday mornings . . .

Painters were working somewhere in the building and something about the odors which drifted through the cracked door stimulated the appetite. Only eleven-fifteen. Much too early for lunch.

Lighting another cigarette, the girl stretched, darted down to the bathroom and from there to the kitchen. The apartment's owners had left the refrigerator on its lowest setting, but she'd turned it up to keep a quart of milk cold. She downed a glass quickly, doused her cigarette in the sink, then returned to her surveillance post, a tall bar stool co-opted from the breakfast counter in the kitchen.

To think there were people who made careers of this! Policemen and detectives and FBI and all the other professional spies. It looked so exciting on television. And so easy. No sooner did a hero get himself strategically placed than some significant piece of action would occur. Television never showed all the boring hours of waiting. Odd how doing nothing was so much more tiring than actual work. Luckily the stool had armrests and a padded back. That helped some. One could always prop elbow on knee, cup chin on hand and rest the eyes a minute. Tiring to keep squinting through that tiny hole . . .

The girl awoke with a guilty start and tried to rationalize that any movement beyond the door would have triggered subconscious alarms even in a sleeping brain. Eleven-forty. Less than fifteen minutes missing and there seemed no change in the landing outside. She shook another cigarette from its crumpled pack and found she had no matches.

Eleven-fifty, eleven fifty-five, and she capitulated to hunger and nicotine. After all, how long could it take to splash cold water on her face, grab a snack, and find matches?

Eight minutes.

Refreshed now and well-supplied with matches, she resolved not to leave the stool again. For once, virtue was instantly rewarded by the rising whine of the elevator. It stopped, the doors opened, and a young, dark-haired man crossed into view, heading for Julie Redmond's door.

He wore polished black boots, white Levi's, and a bright green T-shirt under a white denim jacket. There was something vaguely familiar about his raw good looks, but his eyes were cold and flat as he stared around the landing and he scowled as he jabbed the bell again.

The girl stood silently with her eye pressed to the peephole. Her cigarette burned down to the filter, but there was no time to look around for her ashtray, so she dropped it by her foot and stepped on it.

The dark-haired man rapped sharply on the door, and it must have opened, for he disappeared inside and she heard him say, "Hey, Julie?"

Several minutes passed. The girl was concentrating so intensely upon the main door that the man almost went unnoticed when he first emerged from 3-D's service entrance. There was something markedly stealthy in his bearing. Even more suspicious was how, instead of ringing for the elevator, he pushed open the stairwell door, listened a moment, then slipped silently away.

The watching girl was consumed with curiosity. Was he a thief? Had Julie gotten past, undetected, during one of her absences from the peephole, leaving the front door unlatched?

Cautiously, she tiptoed across the landing. The door of 3-D stood slightly ajar. A gentle push and she was inside. There was no sound from within the apartment.

Across the room, a modern white desk had been turned inside out, papers strewn, its drawers agape. So the man *had* been a thief! Or had he been searching for evidence of his own, too?

The desk was an obvious place to keep things, but the man had left by the service door. Why?

Julie had a devious streak in her and she wouldn't be the first woman to stash papers and photographs in a cookbook or tape them to the bottom of a vegetable bin.

The silence held as the girl moved through the apartment to Julie Redmond's kitchen.

CHAPTER 2

Despite a naïve insistence that we are all one people, people can be (and usually are) divided into many categories. One of the simplest, one that cuts across all orderly groupings of age, sex, race, creed, or national origin, is a basic division of day people from night people.

Day people leap from their beds at dawn's earliest light whether they have to or not and they never stop crowing about glorious sunrises, dewy-fresh morns and how much work they got done before breakfast, as if there were great virtue simply in being up and about when nothing else is stirring but some opportunistic birds and a few sluggish worms.

Night people prefer their days a bit more broken-in. Sunrises strike them as grossly overrated, and anyhow, they'll tell you crossly, sunsets are just as lovely and a hell of a lot more civilized. When's the last time anyone handed you a drink at sunrise?

Unfortunately, schedules and work days are organized chiefly by dawners, and night people learn to accommodate, much as lefties learn to get along in a right-handed world. One learns gratitude for small blessings and to take one's compensations where one can. Which is to say that night people, including police officers, will shamelessly sleep till noon no matter how glorious the morning, if that morning happens to fall on an off-duty weekend.

Lieutenant Sigrid Harald was no exception.

Groggily, she pushed the cutoff button on her alarm clock three times before it finally penetrated that the persistent ringing was telephonic, not horological.

She spoke sleepily into the receiver.

"Still in bed?" demanded the aggressively cheerful voice of a born dawner. "Don't you know what time it is?"

Sigrid resisted an impulse to hang up. Instead, she propped a couple of pillows under her shoulders, pushed away the heavy dark hair and shifted the receiver while examining the clock.

"Are you there?"

"It's only a quarter past ten," she told him resentfully.

"We've been invited to late breakfast, so I'll pick you up in half an hour sharp, okay?"

"Listen, Nauman, I keep telling you: I don't *like* breakfast. Anyhow, it's my weekend off. I was going to sleep till noon and then clean my apartment."

"But now you're awake," Oscar Nauman said, sweet reason itself. "Clean your apartment tomorrow. The sun's shining, birds are singing and we're having a picnic."

"Central Park's full of degenerates," Sigrid objected. "Breakfast is bad enough. Why do I have to put up with flashers, too? I'm off duty, Nauman!"

"Who said anything about Central Park? If you keep arguing, we're going to be late and that's rude. Get dressed. I'll be circling your block in twenty-five minutes."

"Wait!" she cried, awake enough now to remember. "I'm still on call. Give me a phone number where we'll be."

"Will you wear something with color?" he bargained.

"What color?" she asked warily.

"That blue-green suit with the blue ruffled shirt."

"You know my closet better than I do," Sigrid grumbled.

Nauman interpreted that as a promise, and after Sigrid had relayed the number to headquarters, she swung herself out of bed and darted into the bathroom. It took less than five minutes to shower and do up her thick hair into a neat but severe bun at the nape of her neck—all without the aid of mirrors. In fact, Lieutenant Sigrid Harald seldom consulted mirrors except to make sure everything hung together decently: that her skirts were long enough, that a slip didn't show, that her shirts were tucked in, that her face wasn't smudged. At the age of thirteen, she'd decided once and for all that she would forever be too gawky, too tall, and too homely, so mirrors had never become an instrument of vanity.

She could study her face unselfconsciously, noting the too-long neck, her wide gray eyes and dark, level brows, the thin nose and angularities of her face.

She'd never learned to smile at her reflection and continually judged herself by her southern grandmother's antebellum standards. Grandmother Lattimore had raised three stunning daughters and still couldn't accept an ugly duckling granddaughter who refused to turn into a conventionally pretty swan.

Because of Grandmother Lattimore, Sigrid owned two sets of clothes: the serviceable, severely cut, neutral-colored suits she bought for herself, and the brighter, more feminine things her mother, Anne, chose for her to wear whenever they made duty visits South. Sigrid had never enjoyed clothes, but it was easier to wear Anne's choices than listen to Grandmother Lattimore complain that "Sigrid simply isn't trying."

Sigrid considered the Carolina side of her closet peacock feathers for a crow and was annoyed that Nauman seized every opportunity to bully her into them.

Of course, she conceded, as she examined the garments he'd specified, he *was* an artist and had a highly developed color sense, but it was exasperating that having seen her closet only once—it *was* only once, wasn't it? she asked herself, trying to remember how many times he could have been in her bedroom—having seen her closet once, he should remember so much.

Oscar Nauman's artistic reputation was so firmly estab-
lished that he could have retired to the South of France,
painted three or four pictures a year, and lived quite comfortably on the proceeds. But he was too impulsive to hang
onto money and he loved teaching too much—Loves man-
aging everyone's life, more likely, Sigrid thought—to give
up his position as chairman of the art department at Van-
derlyn College. He had to be nearing sixty, but he retained
the vigor and vitality of a much younger man. There were
even times when he made Sigrid feel older than he.

They had met the month before after a homicide in Nauman's department, yet the end of the case had not been the
end of their acquaintance. He kept showing up at odd
times, carrying her off to dinner at disreputable taverns,
marching her around museums and galleries to remedy her
abysmal ignorance of modern art, and appearing on her
threshold with a weird assortment of groceries that he
turned into gourmet meals in her heretofore soup-and-
sandwich kitchen. He was undeterred by her prickly nature, her rudeness, or her insults; and Sigrid had quit trying
to analyze why he persisted.

Or why she hadn't brought herself to sever the relationship once and for all.

Hastily, she donned the blue-green suit he had specified.
The silky wool challis was cut with a slight flare at the
hemline and it swirled around legs which were thin but
finely proportioned. Sigrid frowned at her mirrored image,
noticing only that her slip straps needed shortening. She
was still feeling self-conscious about ruffles at wrist and
neck when Nauman's battered bright yellow sports car
pulled up in front of her apartment building.

"On my first circle, too," he said as he pushed open the
door to let her in. "Punctuality's a rare virtue."

"In a woman, you mean?" she asked. Unfairly, since he
was less chauvinistic than most men she'd met.

"Still cross because I woke you up?" He looked at her
critically. "I told you to leave your hair loose."

"You did not!" Sigrid's hands flew up to protect her
hair. Only last week Nauman had sent her dignity tumbling by pulling out crucial hairpins and strewing them
along the FDR Drive.

"Well, I meant to. What's the point of having hair like yours if you keep it pinned flat all the time? I suppose you want me to stop and put the top up?"

"Not unless this is one of your Indianapolis 500 days."

Sigrid hated fast driving and she didn't think Manhattan traffic should be treated like an amusement park's bumper-car pavilion. Nauman seemed unable to grasp just how embarrassing it was for her, a police officer sworn to uphold the law, to be present during the issuance of so many careless-and-reckless citations. How he managed to hang onto a driver's license anyhow was something she preferred not to question. Knowing Nauman, his good fairy could be anyone—a DMV file clerk or a municipal judge. His circle of acquaintances seemed to range from penthouse duplexes to dimestore basements.

He was on his best behavior now though, driving at a moderate speed and obeying all the laws. Sigrid began to relax. It really was a glorious morning. Just as New Yorkers started thinking hazy skies and low visibility were the norm, along came days like this, when the view from Riverside Drive was stunning and the Palisades across the river shone like the Promised Land in clear sunlight.

She lifted her face to the warm sun, her head tipped back against the headrest, and Nauman found it hard to keep his eyes on the road. Her profile made such a lovely line from her determined chin down the long slender neck. And then she smiled at him and he nearly swerved across two lanes of traffic. Her smile was so rare that one forgot its unconsciously sweet gaiety.

He caught his breath and grinned back. "You need a pet."

Instantly, her smile converted to a scowl and she twisted around to peer behind the seat, almost expecting to find a Great Dane lurking there. Nauman was capable of it.

"I don't want a pet. I don't have time for one. Anyhow, pets aren't allowed in my building."

"These would be and they don't take much time."

"*These?* Pets in the plural? Fish?" She considered the idea of fish. "Aren't they hard to raise? I mean with all the chlorine and chemicals in the city water?"

"Not fish and not—uh-oh, sorry about that!" he apologized, having taken the exit ramp so fast that tires squealed as he braked for the sharp curve.

Sigrid bit her tongue while he concentrated briefly on driving. The backs of his hands were lightly sprinkled with brown age marks, but the hands were still capable—a craftsman's hands, strong and square, yet with the promise of lyrical, gentle touch. Always and entirely against her will, they made her remember those lines, "*Licence my roving hand . . .*" Not that licensing would ever come up. Not that their relationship was anything other than platonic . . .

Oh, blast her undisciplined mind!

Unaware of causing ambivalent thoughts, Nauman spied a parking space and, with a clashing of gears and brakes, whipped into it before a slower sedan could take precedence.

An entrancing yeasty fragrance hung over a sidewalk crowded with amiable shoppers out to enjoy a leisurely Saturday morning. Nauman unfolded his lean frame and handed her out of the yellow MG.

"This is one of the best French bakeries in the world," he said, pulling open the door of an immaculate, heavenly smelling shop. "You won't find better croissants in Paris."

"Paris? *Faugh* on Paris!" sniffed the dark and villainous-faced owner of the shop. "*Dîtes-moi*, Oscar: Where in Paris do you find food fit to eat in the last ten years?"

"There're still a few places."

"*Places*, Oscar?" The man leered suggestively. "Places or *les dames?*" He lapsed into rapid French.

Nauman laughed at those ribald references to the long-gone days of postwar Paris and shook his head ruefully. "*Rien de plus, Jean! Je me fais trop vieux.*"

"You? Ha! You will never be too old, my friend," the man said with a Gallic gesture which included Sigrid as part of his argument.

Fortunately, Sigrid had already headed for the pastry cases and missed both the gesture and Nauman's warning frown. The open car had stimulated her appetite and breakfast was beginning to feel less and less like an idiotic idea. Everything looked as wonderful as it smelled and they filled a large bag with different croissants, brioches, and jam tarts.

From the pastry shop it was only a short drive to a quiet, tree-lined side street. Nauman parked the car, hooked the bag of pastries out of the rear, and led Sigrid down a shallow flight of steps to the basement door of a narrow brownstone.

"*Ciao*, Oscar!" cried a boisterous female voice from within, and the door flew open upon a short, vibrant woman of indeterminate middle age, who stood on tiptoes and pulled Nauman down to her level so that she could plant hearty kisses on either cheek. Her harlequin-shaped glasses had turquoise frames heavily crusted in rhinestones, but otherwise she looked like everyone's childhood image of a little Dutch girl: plump, rosy cheeks, flaxen hair cut straight across in bangs, even a white eyelet blouse and a long peasant skirt of vivid primary colors. Her red wood and leather sandals looked like a space-age version of Dutch clogs.

"Come in! Come in! I hope you bought out Jean's shop. I'm ravenous!"

Nauman held the open bag to her nose and she breathed in the combined aromas of cinnamon, yeast, and peach jam, then beamed at them, still chattering nonstop.

"This is Dr. Gill," Nauman began, but the woman seized Sigrid's hands and said, "Hi! I'm Jill Gill. Feel free to make jokes and bad puns about it. Everyone else does. You must be Sigrid Harald. I wish I could say Oscar's told me all about you, but this morning was the first I've heard. Come along and help bring out the coffee. We're picnicking in the garden. Unless you'd rather have tea? Or maybe cocoa?"

"Coffee's fine," Sigrid murmured, and followed the billowing skirt down a bright hallway which led back to the kitchen and out into a deep walled garden.

Meeting new people socially made Sigrid shy and tongue-tied as a rule, but Jill Gill gave her no time to feel awkward. She was kept so busy bringing out cups and saucers, pots of honey, jam, and butter, a pitcher of milk, and enough breakfast supplies for a dozen people that by the time they were finally settled at the glass-topped patio table at the front of the garden, she felt as if she'd known the woman longer.

There was nothing shy about Dr. Gill. Blunt and plain-spoken, she asked astonishingly personal questions with a child's directness that left Sigrid gasping.

"Stop it, Jilly," said Nauman, lighting his pipe after three croissants, two jam tarts, and three cups of coffee. "She's not a specimen under your microscope."

"Did I sound like I was dissecting?" Dr. Gill looked so genuinely crushed that Sigrid tempered his reproach with a question of her own. "What does he mean by specimen? Are you a scientist?"

"Entomologist. Want to see?" She took another crois-sant, smeared it thickly with butter and jam, and, still munching, led them along a brick walk to the rear of the garden. The entire back wall was given over to a large, fine-meshed wire cage. Within, ground and sides were lined with planters that held a jungle of vines, herbs, and outright weeds.

Sigrid caught her breath. What from the front of the garden had seemed like colorful flowers undulating in a light breeze was in reality dozens of butterflies of every color and size.

On the whole, Sigrid ignored nature. She did not gush over flowers, burble about small animals, or devote much emotion to new moons, first snowflakes, or the like; but so many butterflies in one mass were stunning.

"Where on earth did you get them?"

Pleased by Sigrid's reaction, Jill Gill beamed behind those atrocious rhinestone-studded frames. "From all over," she said, daintily licking the last dollop of jam from her fingers. "Some of them I raised myself, but most were sent to me from all across the country. I write science books for chil-dren and one of 'em—the one about butterflies—hit the bestseller list a few years back. Kids are still sending me specimens from all fifty states."

Sigrid tried to picture butterflies in envelopes, but Dr. Gill disabused her. "They send the chrysalises and cocoons and kids are usually pretty careful about packing them properly.

"I put them all back here so that when they start emerging in the spring, I can catch any unusual specimens. Then every Saturday afternoon, I let the week's hatch go."

Suiting action to words, she folded back the hinged cage top. Hesitantly at first, then with growing confidence, the butterflies fluttered upward; three or four, soon a small cloud lifted in the warm spring air and floated freely into the garden and across the walls. There were several which stayed behind, clinging to the wire, and Dr. Gill showed Sigrid how to slip her hand down until a particularly beautiful insect released its grip and clasped her fingers.

It was a lovely pale green, edged in soft pink with black and gold eyespots on each wing and fully six inches long from top to the long tapering tails of the hind wings.

Too absorbed in the creature to notice how Nauman was looking at the picture they made, Sigrid held her hand high to give it a chance to fly, but it stubbornly clung to her fingertips.

"It's a luna moth," explained Dr. Gill, who *had* noticed Nauman's face. "A night-flyer."

"What's the difference between a moth and a butterfly?"

"Well, the most obvious difference is in antennae and body shape. A butterfly's slenderer and its antennae usually end in little blackjacks at the tips; but a moth's chunkier, more hairy, and the antennae are often feathery. There're other differences, too, of course, but Oscar gets bored when I become technical."

Nauman shrugged, and Jill Gill's sharp blue eyes crinkled merrily through her absurd glasses. "Come alone someday, my dear, and I'll tell you everything you ever wanted to know about lepidoptera but were afraid to ask."

"Perhaps I will," Sigrid said gravely, knowing that when an expert talks about her field, she is never dull.

She was almost sorry when Dr. Gill took the luna from her and transferred it to a tree branch.

"Which kind are you going to give her?" asked Nauman, and Sigrid realized these were the pets he'd threatened her with.

"Can butterflies live in an apartment?"

"Not butterflies—caterpillars."

"Oh, I don't think so," Sigrid said doubtfully, thinking of slimy worms.

They ignored her, discussing the merits of each species.

"The monarch makes the prettiest chrysalis," Dr. Gill said at last. "Like a green-enameled, gold-tipped jewelbox, but it has to be fed milkweed. Do you know what milkweed looks like?" she asked Sigrid. "Almost every abandoned lot all over the city has some growing wild."

Sigrid vigorously disavowed knowing *any* weed by name, but her benefactress was undeterred.

"We'll make it a black swallowtail then. It eats parsley, celery, or fresh dill and you can buy those at any fruit stand along Ninth Avenue."

Everything seemed to go together effortlessly. "No trouble at all," she said over Sigrid's demurrals. "I'm always fixing them for the kids in the neighborhood. They'd rather have a dog, of course, or a cat; but caterpillars are better than nothing if you want something living to care for."

She stuck a small medicine bottle to the bottom of a wide-mouthed gallon glass jar with a dab of Plasticene, added water to the little bottle, then picked several stems of parsley growing in a nearby box. Before standing the parsley in the water bottle, she handed Sigrid a magnifying glass, and there on the leaves Sigrid saw three or four tiny black caterpillars with a yellowish-white saddle mark. They were less than a quarter-inch long and were, if anything, hairy rather than slimy.

"The hair falls off soon and they'll get green with black and yellow stripes as they molt," said the pixyish entomologist, tying a piece of cheesecloth over the mouth of the jar. "Just keep sticking in fresh parsley every few days. When they're as big as your index finger and start crawling off the parsley, add some long bare twigs so they'll have a rigid place to pupate."

Sigrid said it sounded complicated; Nauman told her not to be such a nay-sayer. "It's a perfectly simple, logical process which even a two-year-old could understand."

"Don't you want some, too?" Jill Gill generously asked Oscar.

"Can't," said Nauman. "I'm off to Amsterdam tonight."

"That's right, your exhibition," the woman nodded.

Sigrid suddenly felt as if she'd stepped down on a step which wasn't really there. "Amsterdam?"

"Amsterdam. Didn't I mention it before?"

"No," she said coldly.

"Thought I did. They've gotten together a collection of my stuff and I have to go over and talk about it. Back in a few weeks. Miss me?"

"Certainly not!"

Dr. Gill's round blond head had been following their exchange, switching back and forth as if at a tennis match, when the distant trill of the telephone called her to the house. She went reluctantly, her red shoes flashing beneath the long bright skirt. "If you're going to fight, wait till I get back," she called over her shoulder.

"Are we fighting?" Nauman asked, eying Sigrid.

"Don't be absurd. It just surprised me, that's all."

Nauman looked vaguely disappointed. "I'll miss *you*," he said lightly.

"Miss having someone to bully, you mean." Sigrid's tone was dry.

At the far end of the garden, Jill Gill appeared in the doorway waving the telephone receiver. "It's for 'Lieutenant Harald,'" she called. "Sounds official."

"Oh hell!" said Nauman.

CHAPTER 3

Detective Tildon waited for her in an open doorway on the third floor of the Rensselaer Apartment Building.

Tildon, inevitably called Tillie the Toiler by his colleagues, was a cherubic-faced officer who found it very difficult to make comparisons, draw parallels, formulate theories, or see beyond the obvious; but he was a valuable investigator because he felt his shortcomings keenly and tried to compensate by following the book and taking scrupulous note of every detail uncovered in an investigation. His reports were officialdom's despair, but almost always, somewhere in that mountain of verbiage, the vital clue or damning piece of evidence would have been noted and documented.

Sigrid, aware of her own shortcomings, thought they made an efficient team. She had a clear and usually logical mind which, although she wouldn't admit it, was aided by bursts of sheer intuition; but she lacked Tillie's cheerful bumbling manner, which could so readily disarm witnesses and induce them to say more than they'd often intended.

"Sorry to call you in on such a pretty day, Lieutenant,"

Tillie apologized as she stepped from the elevator, "but things got busy and your name was at the top of the roster."

"It's all right," Sigrid said. Along the way, she'd stopped to change into one of her formless working suits, and all traces of Saturday holidaying were erased. "What do you have so far?"

Tillie consulted his ubiquitous notebook. "Julie Redmond, Caucasian female, early twenties, severe blow to the head. Body discovered around one-fifteen. Divorced and apparently there's a kid—a little boy. No sign of him at the moment.

"I was just about to question the doorman," he concluded, and indicated a gloomy-faced uniformed man who stood by the living-room windows.

Sigrid nodded for him to carry on and made her way through the apartment to a yellow and orange kitchen where the corpse was being examined and photographed *in situ*.

The room seemed crowded as Sigrid entered and stared down at the body. It was too soon to know what Julie Redmond had been like in life, but in death she was still quite lovely. Her features were composed and drained of emotion as she lay on the polished kitchen tiles like a crumpled butterfly carelessly pinned for display. An apricot robe half hid long, shapely legs. There wasn't even much blood apparent, for she lay face up and the crushing blow had been struck from behind. One had to look closely through those soft dark curls to see the shattered skull and drying blood.

For the record, Lieutenant Sigrid Harald was deliberately not looking closely. This was the part she liked least about her job. It was not the sight of blood or gore that bothered her so much, but the grosser obscenity of murder itself. Of a life cut short before its time.

Yet she was aware of sidelong glances from the case-hardened professionals in the room, lab men and precinct officers, who even at this late date still mistrusted women officers. She knew the contempt they'd feel if she showed any vestige of the nausea rising within her, so she forced herself to seem detached—"Cold bitch," thought a sergeant from the local precinct—and looked again.

The girl had been alive only a few short hours ago. She had sat at this table in her bright kitchen, as she drank coffee from a flowered cup and made plans for this day. Was she someone who'd noticed butterflies? That wouldn't matter anymore. Death had made such details irrelevant.

"We haven't printed that yet, Lieutenant!" one of the lab men warned sharply.

"Sorry," Sigrid murmured.

Absentmindedly, she'd almost picked up the weapon, a heavy black flatiron. It was one of a pair which had been used as bookends for the short row of cookbooks now sliding in disarray on the wide windowsill. Sigrid doubted that the rough diamond-patterned handle would yield usable prints but didn't press the point.

"If you wouldn't mind stepping back a little, Lieutenant?" suggested a photographer, his tone bordering on insubordination.

Sigrid turned and chilled him with such a frigid glance that he remembered that the privileges and power of rank extended to female officers, too, and abruptly decided to shoot another camera angle first.

Having examined the body long enough to make her point, Sigrid moved past the lab crew, back down the short hall which led to the rest of apartment 3-D.

As in most of these older apartments in the East Seventies, the living room was high-ceilinged and spacious. It overlooked a narrow strip of trees and flowering bushes and a wider service alley that separated this building from its rear neighbors and allowed the room more light. The dead woman had favored modern furniture, and the sofas and chairs upholstered in apricot velvet must have made a dramatic background for her dark beauty.

The one jarring note was a stark white plastic desk whose open drawers had been thoroughly ransacked. Receipted bills and canceled checks had fallen in drifts upon the floor and a crystal bowl of yellow roses seemed to have been removed from the top of the desk to make room for someone's hasty examination of a box of snapshots.

A hall to the left led to two bedrooms and a bath. The second bedroom had scaled-down furniture, a toy box, and a closet with little boy's clothes. The room was supernally neat except for a pair of fuzzy slippers shaped like small rabbits under the edge of the bed and short blue pants carelessly tossed on the counterpane.

Sigrid opened one of the cabinet doors. She had little experience with children, but there seemed something odd about this room. She tried to visualize the rooms of her cousin's children and remembered random heaps of books, stuffed animals and—since Hilda believed in rampant self-expressiveness—every wall bright with crayoned drawings.

Not a single pencil mark marred the pale blue walls of this child's room. No bits and pieces from games or toys littered the deeper blue carpet, though there were games and toys enough behind the closed cabinet doors, all neatly arranged.

"She really had that kid well trained," Tillie observed from behind her. He had children of his own and Sigrid thought she heard a trace of envy in his tone.

"Any sign of him yet?" she asked.

"The doorman says the lady in 3-B, a Mrs. Cavatori, took him out this morning. The maids over there confirm it. They were going to the circus. The people in 3-A are in Mexico, but that Miss Fitzpatrick's calmed down enough to talk if you're ready."

"Fitzpatrick?"

"She's the one who found the body," reminded Tillie.

Sigrid stepped out into the carpeted vestibule. The building had been well taken care of through the years and wore its age gracefully. She noticed a strong smell of fresh paint. It was not a large building: only four apartments to each floor clustered around a central vestibule. On the left were double doors leading to an enclosed stairwell; on the right, an elevator shaft.

Across the wide vestibule, opposite Julie Redmond's front door, was apartment 3-C, owned by Miss Elizabeth Fitzpatrick. She had discovered the body and then phoned her nephew, her doctor, and her local police station—in that order—before going into mild shock.

As Sigrid started to knock, the door was flung open by

Miss Fitzpatrick's doctor. He was a bouncy little man with a chirping voice and a bustling air of great importance.

"When did they start putting women on homicide cases?" he clucked dissapprovingly. "She'll be asleep in fifteen minutes, so you'd better hurry with your questions. I told her you'd stay until her nephew gets back from the drugstore with her tranquilizers, okay?"

Without pausing for Sigrid's answer, he bounced over to the elevator.

Sigrid shrugged and entered the apartment and immediately stumbled over a hassock.

"*Do* watch your step, young lady!" said an acerbic voice.

Apologizing, Sigrid groped her way forward, half blind in the darkened room. As her eyes adjusted to the dim light, she saw a wispy figure lying on a massive Victorian couch that was piled with small velvet and satin cushions. With her soft white curls caught up in a loose bundle atop her head and her gold-rimmed glasses, Miss Fitzpatrick looked like an illustration from a child's old-fashioned picture book.

All around her, ornately carved tables and curio stands pushed against overstuffed chairs and Tiffany lamps. White lace doilies lay like winter snowflakes on all the arms of the furniture, and linen antimacassars anachronistically protected the upholstered backs from men who no longer slicked their hair with Macassar oil.

Fragile glass figurines and beaded flower arrangements crowded all available surfaces, and on the walls were more bouquets of pressed flowers in gilt frames as well as puritan-faced photographs of unsmiling men and women dressed in turn-of-the-century styles. Around the room, tortoise-framed mirrors with crazed silver distorted everything they reflected.

The Redmond apartment had been starkly modern and so uncluttered as to seem bare, but Miss Fitzpatrick's—

For a moment, Sigrid had the mad impression that she'd blundered into a secondhand-furniture shop.

"I *do* have some nice things, don't I?" the old lady asked proudly, misinterpreting Sigrid's stare. "The only benefit of outliving everyone is that one ends up with all the family heirlooms. But you mustn't waste time gawking. Didn't you hear the doctor? He gave me something to calm my nerves."

She gestured to a dainty spool chair beside the sofa. "Sit there. Or, no—" she countered as she took in the police-woman's tall frame, "perhaps you'd better sit on the love-seat."

Miss Fitzpatrick was quite tiny. Less than five feet high, with fine thin features beneath her topknot of white curls, she examined Sigrid with bright-eyed curiosity.

"I had heard that ladies do everything these days, but investigating murder?" she asked disapprovingly. "Rather young, are you not? Or am I so very old? I'm eighty-seven, you know. Eighty-seven next month, that is. How old are you?"

Reminding herself that she was in charge, Sigrid pulled the sturdiest chair she could see up to the sofa ("Mind you don't scuff the rug!"), smiled pleasantly, and firmly over-rode Miss Fitzpatrick's questions with one of her own. "Do you recall what time you found Mrs. Redmond?"

"Of course I do! I assure you I am not senile!" She glared at Sigrid from her nest of cushions, her chin proudly de-fiant. "It was one-fifteen. I was on my way downstairs to check my mailbox. Disgraceful the way our postal service has deteriorated. When I was a child, Mama could mail her grocery order in the morning and the groceries would ar-rive in the afternoon. Only one delivery a day now and no precise schedule. Still, delivery is usually made by a quarter past one, so that is when I go down for my walk around the block and to pick up my mail. Although these days, it's mostly just my bank statements and circulars addressed to occupant. Attrition, you know. When one lives to be eighty-seven, most of one's friends and relatives are dead.

"Do you know when I felt truly old?" she asked. "It was two years ago when the last person who had known me as a child died. Ninety-three, he was. Now there's no one left who remembers me in my perambulator anymore. A silly thing to care about, is it not?"

For a moment, her proud chin wavered and her bright blue eyes clouded with pain behind the shining glasses.

Sigrid's voice was gentle as she asked, "Exactly how did you discover the body, Miss Fitzpatrick?"

"Her door was ajar. Quite careless, it seemed. An open invitation to thieves. Then I saw that her papers were tossed around on her desk as if it'd been burglarized. However untidy Mrs. Redmond's morals—divorcing her husband, seeing other men—I gathered she was most insistent upon neatness and order." In answer to Sigrid's inquiring gaze, she explained, "No, we had only a nodding acquaintance, but her cleaning woman also cleans for me. A most talkative person," she added.

"As a neighbor though," continued Miss Fitzpatrick, "I felt it my duty to go inside and offer my assistance."

"But weren't you afraid the thief might still be there?" asked Sigrid, who'd warmed to the old woman's crisp spirit.

"One doesn't have to be a policeman to realize how highly illogical that would be."

"Illogical?"

"The *door,* of course. Only the most bungling thief would leave a door half open while he worked. Surely even a police-*woman* would know that?" Miss Fitzpatrick pursed her lips disapprovingly.

"To continue: I entered the kitchen and saw Mrs. Redmond on the floor. I thought she had fainted or perhaps been struck unconscious by the intruder, but she was cold when I touched her."

Again, Miss Fitzpatrick's prim diction faltered. "Quite, quite cold. When one is eighty-seven, death can be a frightening thing."

"And you saw no one?" asked Sigrid.

Miss Fitzpatrick shook her head.

"What about earlier? Did you see or hear anything that might help us?"

"I don't know if it's pertinent, but I did hear her voice raised in anger this morning. The wall between our two kitchens is quite thin. I assure you I have never had the least desire to eavesdrop, but one is sometimes compelled to hear things one would rather not."

As the sedative she'd been given began to take effect, Miss Fitzpatrick smothered a dainty yawn.

"And you heard something this morning?"

"Somewhat earlier I had heard her shrieking at the boy, but that was not unusual. She seemed most unmotherly. Later, I heard her speak quite loudly to the effect, 'He's mine and you can damn well stay away from him!'"

"Did you hear the other person?"

"Only indistinctly. The voice was so low I couldn't even say if it were a man or a woman."

Another ladylike yawn was hidden behind thin, gnarled fingers and Miss Fitzpatrick's eyelids drooped perceptibly.

"And the time'?"

"I'm sorry, Lieutenant, but time has little relevance to me now. All I can be certain of is that it was sometime in midmorning. After six-thirty when I breakfast, but well before twelve-thirty, when I have my lunch."

She yawned again and said politely, "Please excuse me." Then rearranging a handful of ruffled pillows to support her neat white head, Miss Elizabeth Fitzpatrick closed her eyes and was instantly asleep.

Sigrid glanced at her watch. Three o'clock. Almost two hours since the murder had been discovered and all she'd learned was that Julie Redmond had had at least one visitor that morning. Someone with whom she'd quarreled. And who had killed her?

The front door of the apartment opened, and a younger, masculine replica of Miss Fitzpatrick entered, maneuvering through the maze of furniture with familiar dexterity. His eyes were a darker blue and his hair was steel gray instead of white, but he had his aunt's crisp authority and spoke with the same precision as he introduced himself.

"I am Gilbert Fitzpatrick, my aunt's attorney. You should have waited until I was present to question her."

"You thought we might consider her a suspect?" Sigrid asked mildly.

"Of course not! Nevertheless—" He left his objections unvoiced as he examined his watch impatiently. "Where *is* that girl?"

"Did you know Mrs. Redmond?" Sigrid asked.

The lawyer had disappeared down a hallway and seemed not to have heard her. When he reappeared, he carried a puffy silk comforter which he tucked around Miss Fitzpatrick with fussy care. As he gently removed the old lady's glasses, the front door opened again, admitting a young girl who carried notebooks and several high school textbooks which she dumped in the nearest chair.

"Lieutenant Harald, my daughter," he said, regarding the girl with a mixture of pride and admonition.

Eliza Fitzpatrick was fifteen and seemed to have inherited the family traits of small bones and self-assurance although she was still too young and ingenuous to maintain it for long.

She offered her hand formally, then beamed at Sigrid. "A police officer. Neat! Does that mean you're in charge and you can boss around all those men over there? How long have you been a lieutenant?"

"Don't be inquisitive, Eliza!" her father said sharply. "Lieutenant Harald does not have time to answer frivolous questions. Pay attention, please. When your Aunt Elizabeth awakens, this is the medicine the doctor's prescribed, should she feel faint again. You will pack a small case with the overnight things she'll require and I'll pick you both up before dinner."

"Okay," the girl said cheerfully, "but I'll bet you a dollar she won't come home with us."

"Mr. Fitzpatrick," Sigrid interrupted firmly.

"Yes, yes, I heard you before," said the lawyer. "You wanted to know if I was acquainted with Mrs. Redmond?" He took a deep breath. "Certainly not! My aunt had introduced her and we occasionally met in passing, but that was the extent of our acquaintance."

"What about you, Eliza?"

"It was the same for my daughter," said Gilbert Fitzpatrick brusquely and held the door open for Sigrid. "Shall we go before we disturb my aunt?"

Sigrid had no choice but to follow him, but she'd noticed the way Eliza's chin had come up defiantly when her father denied any real knowledge of Julie Redmond, and she made a mental note to see the girl again when Mr. Fitzpatrick wasn't around.

CHAPTER 4

Once more Detective Tildon met Sigrid in the open doorway to apartment 3-D.

"The doorman said her ex-husband was here this morning," he reported significantly. "Arrived around ten-fifteen, left about eleven. And 3-B just came back. Mrs. Cavatori. She's got the Redmond kid with her, cute little guy. I told her you'd be right in to see them."

"You'd better come, too, since you're the child expert," Sigrid said. She crossed the vestibule and rang the bell at 3-B. It was opened almost immediately by a plump, vibrant woman in her early sixties.

"Mrs. Cavatori? I'm Lieutenant Harald and this is Detective Tildon. May we come in?"

"*Ma sicuro,* Lieutenant, certainly; but please—the boy—he must not hear. A moment only, *per favore.*"

She closed the door behind them and gestured toward chairs in the living room; then carrying a toy clown, she bustled away to the rear of the apartment and a moment later they heard her voice, cheerful and loving, mingled with that of a young child.

Located on the street side of the building, the Cavatori apartment was rather larger than the rear ones of Julie Redmond's or Miss Fitzpatrick's, and the mood was different again. The decor was more formal, yet there was a warm, homey feeling.

Money—lots of money—had probably been spent on the rooms they could see from where they stood, but it was money spent for comfort, not ostentation. The furnishings were old, solid, and of obvious quality; and everything seemed cherished. All the glass, from window panes to Venetian ashtrays, sparkled and the gleaming wood surfaces exuded an old-fashioned smell of beeswax and lemon oil.

A long, intricately carved, marble-topped chest ranged against one wall and a large bowl of anemones and jonquils on the nearer end almost obscured the groupings beyond. Just above the chest top, a crystal rosary hung from the wall in graceful loops, its gold crucifix barely clearing the flame tip of the single votive candle. Several silver-framed photographs—two or three turn-of-the-century portraits, a couple of informal family snapshots, and one of a dark-haired youth—clustered about the candle. Across the room, dark red drapes had been looped back to let in afternoon sun across thick white carpets.

Mrs. Cavatori returned and clucked and bustled as she scolded them for not sitting. A maid trailed in her wake with a heavily laden tray of coffee and sweet pastries. In Luisa Cavatori's experience, few were the occasions that couldn't be eased with food or drink. No visitor had ever gone away from her home hungry.

She seemed like a classic Italian signora—plump, bossy, with expressive black eyes and excited gestures—and Sigrid recognized that the woman was incapable of sitting if there were the remotest possibility of a guest's hunger or thirst.

Resigned, she and Tillie accepted cups and saucers, then had to wait until the rapid burst of questions and exclamations about Julie Redmond's death had subsided before Sigrid could interpolate her own questions.

"What time did I last see Julie? Only this morning, of course. About ten-thirty. When I take Timmy to the circus.

Povero bimbo! All week he has been so excited for this day. He is like the grandson we never had, and Julie has no nursemaid, so I borrow him often. All week I have promised him the circus and today I take him."

"Did Mrs. Redmond seem upset or worried about anything?"

"Worried? No. Upset? She is easy to upset. Timmy had spilled cereal on his new pants and she was, as you say, upset about that, but—"

An expressive shrug and a humorous downward tug of her lips showed how little importance Mrs. Cavatori attached to that domestic crisis and Sigrid recalled Miss Fitzpatrick's remarks about the dead woman's frequent outbursts at the child.

"No, when we left, she was sitting with another cup of coffee. She was like you, Lieutenant," Mrs. Cavatori scolded. "Too skinny and all the time not a drop of cream or sugar in her coffee."

Her plump hands advanced with the cream pitcher once more and Sigrid hastily moved her cup out of range.

"Had she said anything about expecting visitors or going out later?"

"There was a dress at Saks she saw in the paper. I told her not to hurry. I would give Timmy his nap. Since he was a baby we have a little bed for him here."

Tillie's neat shorthand covered several notebook pages as, with only a little encouragement, the woman filled in their picture of Julie Redmond, beginning with her marriage to Karl Redmond four years ago.

Redmond's father had been a courtly old-country gentleman who had owned one of those hole-in-the-wall shops down on Canal Street, one of those shops whose grimy façade hid a sultan's glittering treasure trove of cut and uncut gems.

Old Mr. Redmond had anglicized his name, but otherwise he'd been as unpretentious as his shop and he had run his business with old-fashioned methods, treating his shimmering wares as casually as a grocer might treat cheeses and pickles. It had provided a comfortable, honorable living and should have done the same for his only son.

Old Mr. Redmond had not approved his son's choice of

wife, explained Mrs. Cavatori, but he had given them the apartment across the hall as a wedding gift, which was how she had met the Redmonds.

"So beautiful Julie was. Like a *principessa* from a fairy story. But I do not think she had a nice family when she was little."

In other words, Julie Redmond had beauty, but her antecedents were implicit in her brother.

"That Mickey Novak! He has bad eyes. Cold. They look at you and they do not see a person. They see how much money you have and if he can get some of it."

Sigrid knew the type. "Did he visit his sister often?"

Mrs. Cavatori shrugged disdainfully. "Only since last year. Before that, he was in prison."

Detective Tildon looked at Sigrid expressively and added an extra question mark to Mickey Novak's name.

Mrs. Cavatori intercepted their look. "You think him?" she asked. "*É possibile*. Many times they fight together. Not open, you understand, but underneath—like two dogs that circle around each other. Once he called her an ugly name and she slapped him. Hard. He looked like he could kill her, but I was there and Timmy. Maybe today—?"

Sigrid murmured that they'd certainly be talking to Mickey Novak, but for the present, if Mrs. Cavatori would go on with her narrative?

The woman nodded.

"Julie and Karl, they were not happy together. Who can say why? Both good people, but Karl is quiet and not bossy and Julie—such a hard worker, never a speck of dirt in her house, Timmy always dressed so nice—but maybe she needed Karl to tell her to shut up sometimes.

"You, Lieutenant, you are a professional woman, but you listen when your husband speaks, no?"

"I'm not married," Sigrid said stiffly.

"Ah," said Mrs. Cavatori sympathetically. "Never mind, Lieutenant, you are still a young woman."

Tillie kept his eyes fastened on his notebook.

"When were the Redmonds divorced?" Sigrid asked.

"Last spring. Everything went wrong for them then. First Mr. Redmond, then the business, then the divorce."

Mrs. Cavatori was unclear about all the details of how the business failed, but old Mr. Redmond's death the previous spring was still fresh in her memory.

"The police came then, too, to talk to Karl and Julie, so maybe you know all about it, Lieutenant?"

Sigrid didn't, but it was a story which had become depressingly familiar these last few years: diamond merchants who still believed it was safer to carry a duke's ransom around town in their trousers pockets than to hire an armed guard.

"Half a million dollars' worth of diamonds he had that day. All gone! And no insurance. Karl tried, but he could not keep the business going with such a loss. All, all poor Karl did lose—father, business, even his wife and home. Like her brother Julie was then, knowing exactly how much she can get from Karl and taking everything!"

Mrs. Cavatori's dark eyes flashed disapproval and Sigrid was puzzled. "If you felt that way—"

"Why did I stay her friend?" She held her smooth hands out helplessly.

"With Karl, she was greedy, but who knows what happens between husband and wife? With Vico and me she was always very nice, very good." She sighed. "Could I stop the divorce? No. And we love Timmy. My Vico, you should see his face when Timmy climbs onto his lap. Could we turn our back on him because his mother and father cannot keep their holy vows?"

The marriage had been stormy from the beginning; and Timmy's birth, coming so quickly, had only aggravated the situation. In Mrs. Cavatori's opinion, Julie had literally driven Karl into the arms of the girl so quickly named in her divorce suit. It sounded like taking candy from an unresisting baby the way Julie had wound up with the apartment, custody of Timmy, and an adequate child-support allowance. Especially since Mrs. Cavatori suspected that Julie had broken their marriage vows first.

"Law is not always justice, no, Lieutenant?"

"If she had someone else and Redmond cared more for the boy, why didn't he petition the court for a change in custody?"

"He has no more money for lawyers. Besides, what can be provided? He lives openly with another, but not Julie. A nun she is since the divorce. Only she and Timmy sleep in that apartment this last year. Who knows what happened? Perhaps her lover does not want her free. Perhaps she does not want him. Who can say?" Her plump, beringed hands sketched bafflement in the air.

"Or perhaps she does not wish to lose the money for Timmy. No alimony did she get when they divorced. Just a lump sum and the apartment. She was young, able to work. A secretary she was before, yet she does not work. Her lover must be very rich, for she has everything and still—"

Her words broke off as the door closed in the vestibule and a thin, elderly man hesitated in the archway.

Mrs. Cavatori quickly rose and went to him, flooding him in rapid Italian as she took his jacket and led him over to the room's most comfortable chair.

"*Mi scusa,* Lieutenant," she said, introducing him to Sigrid and Tillie. "This is my very bad husband who does not listen to his doctor or to me, who goes for long walks when he should be resting."

"Only to the park, Luisa. Only to sit in the sun." Vico Cavatori smiled at them and his calm brown eyes invited Detective Tildon to share a male solidarity before clucking maternalism.

The maid had reappeared without being summoned and this time her enameled brass tray held a glass of water and a pill bottle. Still scolding, Mrs. Cavatori extracted a pill for him. It was obvious that she adored him and that her household centered around this emaciated old man.

In earlier years, Vico Cavatori had been a vigorous, wiry man with glowing café au lait skin. Poor health—heart condition? wondered Sigrid—made him sallow now. Thin white hair lay like soft spun silk on his head and through it, Sigrid saw dark brown age marks on his scalp, a confirmation of those on his face and the backs of his hands. She realized that he probably wasn't much older than his wife, but his extreme fragility and white hair were in such contrast to her vivid coloring and personality that he seemed years older. Only his eyes, kind and wise, were ageless.

You could trust those eyes, thought Sigrid; feel safe confiding anything, knowing he wouldn't judge. Yet you would hesitate to bare your soul completely, so afraid you'd be of disillusioning a man who looked as if he'd walked the earth nearly seventy years and seen no evil. He radiated sheer goodness and his quiet smile was seraphic.

"They told me of Julie," he said, speaking lightly accented English as a courtesy to guests in his home. "Is Timmy all right?"

"He was with me," Mrs. Cavatori assured him. "And now he plays with his toy clowns in his little room here."

"Good, good." His eyes caressed his wife as she handed him a cup of espresso. Sigrid and Tillie declined refills, and when the maid departed with their empty cups, Tillie unobtrusively trailed out after her, carrying the second tray.

"I'll try not to take much more of your time," Sigrid told them.

"But you wish to know if I heard or saw anything," said Vico Cavatori, shaking his head, "I regret that I must disappoint you. Soon after Luisa left, I had a guest. When he had gone, I went out to lunch myself. It was warm, so I stopped to sit in the sun."

"Who came, Vico?" Mrs. Cavatori asked curiously.

"No one of importance, *cara.*"

"I'm afraid I'll need his name," Sigrid said. "Perhaps he saw something."

"I'm sure not," said the old man firmly. "We spoke in the vestibule until the elevator came and there was nothing to see."

"Nevertheless," Sigrid insisted.

Resigned, Cavatori sank back in his chair. "It was Karl Redmond."

"*Karl?*" exclaimed Mrs. Cavatori. "*Ma, perchè?* Why?"

"He is starting again with his own jewelry," he explained, as much to Sigrid as to his wife. "Not real stones or diamonds like his father, but things the young can buy. Costume jewelry. And these."

From the pocket of his soft blue cardigan, he took a

small box. Inside were several colorful plastic and brass discs of a curious design.

In partnership with a distant cousin, Vico Cavatori owned a quietly prosperous company which specialized in imported sportswear. Since his latest heart attack, all business activities had been stringently proscribed by his doctor and Luisa Cavatori was torn between scolding him for this small disobedience and her natural curiosity.

"Why, it is our symbol!" she exclaimed, turning one of the tiny oval discs in her plump fingers. "See," she said to Sigrid, pointing out the intertwined letters which formed the company name. "But what's it for, Vico?"

"Zipper pulls on ski jackets to start with. Karl says the young like to wear brand names, on necklaces, bracelets, even tee shirts. Why not ours? So he has made our trademark in a fresher, brighter way.

"'Plastic?' I ask him, and he says, 'Why not? It is of our times. It is fashion.' What do you think, Lieutenant?"

"I do not think the lieutenant is interested in fashion," Mrs. Cavatori said dryly, making Sigrid suddenly wish she hadn't changed from the blue-green suit into this shapeless gray pant-suit.

The older woman was like a summer bouquet in a flowery silk dress that flattered her vigorous coloring. "It is pretty, Karl's design; but he should have taken it to Mario, not you."

"I am his friend, Luisa. He does not know Mario."

"And because you are his friend, he thinks to get around you first!" she said scornfully. "Let him show it to Mario. If Mario thinks it will sell more jackets, *bene*; if not—" She shrugged dismissively.

"Ah, Luisa," he said gently.

But she was angry now. "No! Why should you buy this? Why should he have money from you to support that— that—" She lapsed into a torrent of Italian which even Sigrid understood to be abuse of Karl Redmond's mistress.

"*Basta!*" said her husband sternly. "Enough, Luisa! You embarrass the lieutenant."

Instantly, Mrs. Cavatori's anger evaporated and she held out her hand in contrition. "*Mi dispiaccio, caro mio, ma—*"

"Papa Vico!" shrieked a happy little voice and they all turned as a young child danced across the thick carpets in stocking feet to fling himself upon the frail old man.

"Gently, gently!" Mrs. Cavatori warned, but her husband opened his arms and Timmy Redmond snuggled into their curve and settled himself firmly on Cavatori's lap.

He was an attractive child, not quite three, with straight sandy brown hair and clear blue eyes.

"I-me seed a c'own," he confided to Mr. Cavatori. "He had funny shoes."

The boy hopped down and lurched across the carpet, rolling and tumbling in high clown style until he suddenly banged into Detective Tildon, who'd returned from the kitchen unnoticed and sat quietly in one of the side chairs just inside the room.

Abruptly, Timmy cringed away from the smiling detective's friendly hand up and with a fearful yelp, almost tripped in his terrified retreat to Vico Cavatori's arms.

Tillie was crushed. Children had always trusted him.

"It is not your fault, Detective Tildon," Mrs. Cavatori explained cluckingly. "Timmy is shy with all men. Only with my Vico does he feel safe."

"Have you told him?" Sigrid asked quietly as the old man gentled the child.

"That his mama has gone away and that he will come live with us for a while, *si*." Her dark eyes yearned toward the boy. "He is too young to understand more."

At Sigrid's voice, Timmy peeped around the corner of the chair and she smiled at him diffidently. Children were definitely not her forte and she'd assumed that Tillie would be the one to extract any information Julie Redmond's son might possess. She took a deep breath and essayed an awkward, "Was the circus fun, Timmy?"

Immediately, he buried his face in Cavatori's shoulder and refused to answer.

Mrs. Cavatori bristled defensively. "You *cannot* ask him questions!"

"You and he may have been the last to see his mother alive," Sigrid said coldly.

"Then ask me! Timmy is a baby!"

"Even babies are observant, ma'am," offered Tillie from experience with his own. "Timmy seems like a bright little kid."

"Hear how they talk of you, Timmy," said Mr. Cavatori lightly with an admonishing glance at his wife, who subsided unwillingly. "They think you can't remember this morning," he continued gently. "They think the circus put everything out of your mind. Did it?"

Timmy's head was still pressed firmly against Cavatori's frail shoulder, but they saw it give an almost imperceptible shake.

"Then tell Papa Vico about this beautiful morning," he coaxed. "Was the sun shining when you woke up?"

A faint nod.

"Did you remember about the circus when you woke up?"

A firmer nod and a slight relaxing of tension. Like a flower uncurling in the sun, the little boy gradually released his tight hold and lay against Cavatori's chest with his eyes fixed trustingly on those finely etched features.

Soon he was chattering freely about the morning's adventures. The circus dominated, of course, but under Cavatori's skillful leading, a picture of Julie Redmond's last morning emerged.

They had been alone in the apartment. Mommy had spoken twice on the phone but he didn't know to whom. The boy was a good mimic. Quite unconsciously came the image of an impatient, short-tempered woman. She hadn't praised Timmy for dressing himself, only scolded because he couldn't yet tie his shoes.

"Me no *can*," he told Vico with a troubled mixture of sorrow and frustration.

"You will someday," Cavatori assured him. "I couldn't tie my own shoes till I was this many." He held up seven fingers.

Timmy was impressed. "I-me this many," he said, holding up two fingers.

There was a brief discussion of how many fingers he would be upon his birthday, two months away, then Cavatori led him back to breakfast.

Timmy was reluctant to discuss the spilled cereal and Mrs. Cavatori had to help out. "It was an accident, *caro*, you did not mean to."

"'Timmy, you *bad* boy! You no go circus!'" he mimicked sternly. His wide blue eyes filled with tears and his lips trembled, but Vico Cavatori hugged him and patted his cheek.

"Then Mama Luisa came," he comforted the boy, "and then what happened?"

"Clean pants," Timmy explained, "and 'Hurry, hurry, Timmy, we be late!' I-me say, 'Bye-bye, Mommy,' and Mommy say, 'Bye-bye, Timmy. You besa good boy.'" His voice, imitating, was high-pitched and far away, as if she'd called from the kitchen.

His blue eyes were blissful as he smiled at Mrs. Cavatori and told Vico that she'd lifted him up to the elevator. "An' I-me puncha button!"

"Is that sufficient, Lieutenant?" asked Cavatori. His voice sounded fatigued.

"Excellent, thank you," Sigrid told him. "Mrs. Cavatori, could you say when, precisely, you and Timmy left the apartment?"

"Ten-thirty? Perhaps a minute or two before, who can say? We hurried because the circus was to begin at eleven. Please now, Lieutenant Harald, no more questions," she said anxiously. The doctors had been explicit after Vico's last heart attack. "No emotional stress," they had said.

She looked at her husband's drawn face. "These two should both rest before dinner."

"Of course," said Sigrid. As she rose, tall and unsmiling, Timmy shrank back into Vico Cavatori's arms. "One last detail for now, Mr. Cavatori: What time did you see Karl Redmond enter the elevator?"

"Around eleven. More precise I cannot be."

His mild eyes followed the police officer's tall figure as she and the detective were shown out. An odd one, that girl. Awkward and graceless inside her body, he thought. Not like his Luisa, who knew herself loved and whose flashing temperament had warmed the long years of their marriage.

Luisa Cavatori returned from the front door and smiled indulgently. Timmy had fallen asleep in Vico's arms and Vico looked almost as drowsy. She took the child from him in her own strong arms and whispered to her husband, "Come, *caro*. A soft bed now for both my men."

Vico Cavatori nodded wearily, but instead of going to his own room, he followed her down the hall to the room they had furnished for Timmy.

The boy whimpered a little in his sleep when she pulled up the soft coverlet and her face grew angry as she knelt by his bed. "It is not right such a young one should cry like this in his sleep."

"Shh," whispered Cavatori, stroking her hair. Still dark and shining it was, with almost no gray.

Luisa caught his hand in hers and kissed it.

"What will happen to him, Vico, with Julie dead? He is so afraid of Karl. And that girl he lives with—what kind of home is that for our Timmy?"

"Don't borrow trouble, Luisa *mia*. First we will call Mario, then Karl. He must be told of Julie. Little by little, all things come."

Luisa Cavatori smiled at her husband's familiar phrase and allowed herself to hope.

CHAPTER 5

South of West Houston Street and bisected by West Broadway lies SoHo, third-generation Bohemia. Not quite as raffish as Greenwich Village in its heyday, nor as free-wheeling as the East Village during the Sixties, SoHo is a yeasty warren of streets, unexpected alleyways, and old two- to five-story brick buildings. These buildings had once housed a variety of light industries whose products were now turned out cheaper in Taiwan or Korea or even in sparsely unionized pockets of the sunbelt far from New York.

Sporadic rent from a struggling artist is better than no rent at all and landlords had discovered that artists are less uptight about heat, plumbing, and missing window panes; so when Greenwich Village became too expensive, the artists and craftsmen had moved south, hungry for cheap loft space—"and cheap Chinese food," gloated one destitute potter. There, on the northwest edge of Chinatown, they'd found both.

While Karl Redmond ran down two flights to answer the telephone in the shop, Bryna Leighton poked around the bottom of one of the cardboard cartons which had held their late lunch and, with expertly held chopsticks, delicately extracted the last prawn from the remaining fried rice.

Chinese food wasn't supposed to be fattening, but if she kept on like this—! At least she'd transferred the cashews from her half of the chicken dish to Karl's paper plate. He could use the extra calories.

Worry and frustration—and deprivation, too, she noted thoughtfully—had him hollow-eyed these days. If something didn't break soon, she'd insist that he share some of her vitamin tablets. She was healthy enough to spare them, even though there had been dull twinges through her lower back all day.

Ignoring them, she moved heavily to the sink in the curtained-off alcove they called a kitchen and rinsed out two mugs. From the corner of her eye, she saw scurrying legs disappear behind the drainpipes and she reached for the insecticide. A confused fear of fluorocarbons and environmental poisoning stayed her hand. Wait until they get really bad, she decided, and remembered that she'd seen tansy growing wild in a vacant lot off Spring Street. Wasn't tansy supposed to be a natural bug repellant? And safe?

She filled the tin kettle and struck a match to the burner. The stove was an enormous gas range salvaged from a Brooklyn aunt's next-door neighbor and moved here in the back of a friend's van. "My niece will take anything if it's free," Aunt Kitty said; and during that period, the neighbors called her first before they called Saint Joseph's Mission.

As a result, this big empty space was as comfortable as castoff appliances and furniture could make it. Bryna had painted everything white—pipes, floor, walls, and woodwork. Worn carpets and makeshift screens defined the areas, separating bedroom from living space. The bed she now shared with Karl was an old sofa bed left permanently open; and over by the windows, three more couches set at right angles to each other made an inviting place for a dozen or more people to sit and talk.

The teakettle whistled softly. Bryna poured boiling

water over their teabags, added a spoonful of honey to Karl's cup, and carried both mugs back to the solid oak table that they had planned to scrape down and refinish.

She heard Karl's foot on the stair, then a tinkle as the shop door opened and a customer drew him back. She waited placidly, no longer irritated by that placidity. It was hard to remember how once she'd run and flitted from task to task, full of plans for every facet of their lives, eager to begin new projects. Now she planned nothing beyond the next action and the unstructured rhythm only vaguely worried her.

She remembered a science fiction story she'd read once in which a man went about buying up his friends' extra time. Occasionally she wondered if someone had contracted to buy hers. She seemed to procrastinate endlessly these days—nothing accomplished, projects abandoned before they were well begun—had she sold her time and somehow forgotten about it?

Hardly—she smiled, with a flash of her old humor. If she'd exchanged her productive time for money, they wouldn't be worried about meeting all the bills, would they?

The shop bell tinkled again and Karl returned, an odd expression on his face, half excited, half what? Ashamed? Stunned?

"Buyers?" asked Bryna.

"Lookers," he said, but without the usual bitterness. He took the mug of tea she handed him, looked at it blankly, and then set it back on the table.

"Julie's dead," he said. "That was Luisa Cavatori on the phone. Julie was murdered this morning. Somebody hit her with one of those flatirons we bought up at Haines Falls."

"What about Timmy?" Bryna whispered.

"Timmy?" For a moment he was puzzled by her question, then his face cleared. "No, he's okay. Luisa had taken him to the circus this morning. Must have happened right after I was there."

A small fear made Bryna shiver.

"It's weird," he said, "but while Luisa was talking, all

I could think about was that now we can get married. Now. Today. Or whenever we can get a license and a priest, right?"

Bryna was silent.

"I guess that sounds pretty callous, doesn't it?" He studied her face.

"No," she said and touched his hand. "Not really. If I were honest, I'd admit I won't miss having to pay her money we don't have every month."

For the first time in weeks, anticipation stirred her. "We'll have to find a cot. Didn't Pete and Gina have one they wanted to get rid of? We can rearrange the couches and everything so he can have part of a window."

"What are you talking about?"

"About making a place here for Timmy."

"No!"

"Karl, he's your son!"

"He hates me!" Karl said tightly. "He screams every time I try to touch him. How can we have him here now anyhow?"

"We could manage."

But even as she said it, she thought about her lethargy, the drifting of her days.

Karl saw her hesitation and pounced on it. "No, sweetheart. Luisa thinks—and I agree—that it'd be better for Timmy not to have to cope with too many changes all at once. She and Vico are good with him. God knows he loves them better than he loves me. They'll keep him until things get settled down. Maybe after a while, but not now."

He cupped her face with his hands. "Not now," he repeated, and it was almost a plea.

"Okay," she said, remembering that, after all, she had no right to push.

He stood up suddenly. "Lord, I almost forgot!"

He slapped the pockets of his jeans and located a slip of paper. "Luisa gave me the address of Vico's partner, Mario Fuselli. Vico's arranged an appointment at five-thirty. What'd I do with those zipper pulls?"

Bryna watched as he located the samples they'd worked up together.

She was the craftsman, he the one with ideas to sell them. Funny the way their roles had changed. When they first met, he was the drifting one with no thought beyond the day. Drained by his father's brutal death and Julie's emasculating coldness, he had let her rearrange his life, unresisting.

Now he overflowed with plans and schemes to produce and market not just zipper pulls but a whole line of popular fashion jewelry. And she, who should have caught fire from his blazing excitement, could barely muster interest in the day-to-day running of the shop.

Karl peered in a mirror and rubbed his chin. "Better shave," he said, and headed for the small cubicle of a bathroom in the far corner of the flat.

"Luisa said Fuselli's old-fashioned. That means suit and tie. Just like the old days. 'The customers can wear anything they want,' Pop used to tell me, 'but they don't trust a jeweler who dresses like a soda jerk.'"

Bryna heard the pain underneath his light words and helped him find a clean shirt. The unsolved murder still haunted him.

Karl and his father had been so close. How could he have allowed such an abyss to open between himself and his own son?

He looked like a stranger when he emerged from the screens around their bedroom in polished shoes and precisely knotted tie. Good tailoring never lost its shape and the suit still fitted well despite his weight loss. He had half a dozen of those suits left over from the more prosperous days before she knew him.

They had met by chance. Bryna had heard that a jewelry store was unloading the remnants of its stock at rock-bottom prices and had gone with a silversmith friend, hoping for bargains.

She'd been touched by the sandy-haired man with hurt in his eyes, who showed them what was left and seemed indifferent to the value of his stock.

"But that's too cheap!" she'd exclaimed after Karl told her the price of an odd lot of aquamarines.

He had shrugged when she said he was cheating himself; so after checking out his other prices, Bryna had talked him into letting her handle the sale for a percentage of the extra profits.

Two weeks later, Julie had begun divorce proceedings and Karl moved into the loft with Bryna.

She had been scraping by comfortably enough alone; with Karl there, money was much tighter. Gentle, undemanding lovemaking had helped him recover his initiative and he soon pulled his weight in the shop; but meeting Julie's monthly demands strained them to the limit.

At first, Karl had paid whatever she asked; then, as life took hold of him again in the months following his father's death, he'd become resentful of Julie's whiplash scorn, of the way she made him feel that the sum the judge had set for child support was his tribute to her, not his son.

Even harder to endure was the way she'd turned Timmy against him. He'd virtually quit seeing the child, so unhappy and strained were their occasional outings.

It would be different now, Bryna thought. Julie was dead and already some of the tension seemed to be gone from Karl's eyes.

He touched her hair, breaking her reverie. "Will you be okay, sweetheart?"

"I'll be fine," she said, smiling, and followed him downstairs.

At the bottom of the stairway, another twinge of pain rippled through her, but Karl was already through the front door and she wouldn't have called him back for that anyhow.

He walked briskly, eager for the chance this meeting with Vico's partner could make; and perhaps it was that confident tilt of his head that took her over to her workbench.

Despite those back pains, she suddenly felt lighter than she had in weeks. As if her lost energy were returning. She felt like tackling something physical and vigorous, scrubbing floors or washing windows perhaps.

Instead, she picked up a necklace she'd abandoned last month and immediately saw the solution to the design flaw which had caused her to cast it aside.

She sorted out her tools and was instantly absorbed.

CHAPTER 6

As Sigrid and Tillie crossed the landing, they saw two attendants wheeling the loaded stretcher from the service entrance of 3-D.

"Oh, there you are, Harald," said Cohen, an assistant Medical Examiner, who'd just authorized removal of the body. "Wait a minute, you guys."

The attendants paused stoically, and Cohen motioned to Sigrid as he lifted the sheet and drew it back.

"It'll be in my report, but I thought you'd like to know about this now." He pulled aside the collar of Julie Redmond's apricot robe and pushed back a handful of dark hair as if it were nothing more than a window dummy's polystyrene wig. "See the abrasion on the neck? Looks like a necklace or something was yanked off; probably a thin chain the way the skin's torn."

"Before or after she was killed?"

"Oh, definitely after. Wasn't any bleeding there." He flipped the sheet back over the dead girl's face and waved the stretcher on into the elevator.

"What about the actual blows that killed her?" asked Sigrid.

"Looks like only one; and offhand, I'd say a right-handed person of average strength. Nothing fancy. She was probably sitting there at the breakfast table with her back turned and whoever it was just grabbed the nearest object—in this case, one of those flatirons on the windowsill—and let her have it."

"Any guess as to when yet? We have one person so far who saw her alive around ten-thirty."

"Yeah? Well, that'll help narrow it down. I was going to say nine-thirty at the earliest, 'cause she was lying in the sunshine and that'd slow down the cooling," said Cohen, who cultivated a laconic manner. " 'Course, that tile floor ... they found her at one-fifty, y'know, and by the time we got here ... "

He did a few mental calculations. "Okay. Say any time between ten-thirty and twelve-thirty at the absolute latest unless I tell you different in my report."

With a friendly salute, Cohen followed the stretcher into the elevator.

Sigrid and Tillie re-entered the Redmond apartment and were immediately waylaid by one of the local precinct men. Young Officer Crowell was enthusiastic, ambitious, and at the moment, positively pink-cheeked with his good fortune.

"I was checking in with my sergeant," he explained, "when I noticed the wires."

The telephone in question was a white extension in Julie Redmond's bedroom. As Officer Crowell had discovered, it did indeed carry a simple tap which was connected to a tape recorder in the top drawer of the bedside stand.

"Very nice, Officer—?"

"Crowell, ma'am. Freddy—I mean, Frederick Crowell."

"Detective Tildon," said Sigrid, dryly formal, "please make a note that this device was the discovery of Officer Frederick Crowell."

Tillie grinned and Crowell grew even pinker.

The photographer was summoned from the next room and after appropriate pictures had been taken of the apparatus, Sigrid pressed the recorder's rewind button. When it cut off, she pressed *Play*. There was a sound of a telephone bell, a man answered, then the dead girl spoke from the drawer.

"Hullo, George, darling!" Her voice was light and breathless with a studied effect of sensuality.

"Oh, Christ!" said the man, his voice dropping in resignation.

"Is that any way to say hello, darling?"

"What do you want, Julie?"

"You, George. Just you."

The man made a rude sound and the girl's laughter rippled through the room.

"Damn it, Julie! We went through all this four years ago. It's too late now, doll. You made your choice."

"But it was the wrong one, darling. You're not going to hold it against me forever, are you? Admit it, we all make mistakes, don't we?"

Silence.

"I said, don't we, George?" A sardonic taunt crept into her voice now, as of a cat toying with a mouse she hadn't quite decided to eat.

"Why do you keep bringing it up?" the man asked angrily.

"What's the point of—?" There was a reflective pause, then a low, incredulous, "Damn! Are you taping this?"

"Now why would I do a silly thing like that?" she began. She was too late. The man had hung up.

Laughter rippled again and there was the sound of the drawer being opened as she'd stopped the tape. Nothing else was on the cassette.

"He knew about the tap," exclaimed Officer Crowell.

Sigrid nodded. "So it would seem."

"Blackmail?" wondered Tillie.

"Instead of the lover Mrs. Cavatori thought she had? Possibly. That could explain how she lived so well without working."

Sigrid checked the other drawers in the nightstand. "No tapes here, but others could be stashed around the apartment. Keep your eyes open."

They began a cursory search. Officer Crowell was assigned Julie Redmond's collection of rock music and told to make sure a Devo label hadn't been stuck over a home-made tape as camouflage.

As they moved into the living room, they noticed a man in white coveralls speaking to the remaining technicians who were waiting for Sigrid to dismiss them.

The photographer signaled to her. "Mr. Gilchrist here has some info, Lieutenant."

A vigorous fifty, Gilchrist had medium brown skin, a pencil-thin moustache, and the ability to add two plus two without a calculator. He made the shift from male police officer to the officer's female superior without flicking an eyelash.

"It's like this, Lieutenant," he said, a light lilt of the Caribbean in his voice. "I got the contract to paint this building, yes? Hallways, main lobby, and stairwells."

Despite the easygoing lilt, Gilchrist was a thorough professional. He had told his crew to save the stairs for last, he explained, because they'd had to cart extension ladders up and down and he hadn't wanted to risk scarring the walls. Retouching cost time and money.

The stairwell's walls, ceiling, and rails had been finished yesterday; nothing was left except the treads and risers themselves and even those had been painted almost down to the third floor the evening before when his crew had knocked off for the weekend.

"But my old woman's gone visiting our grandbabies over in Jersey, so I decided to come on back this morning and finish up here myself. Got another job starting Monday morning and this little bit's not worth tying up a man all day, and that's what it'd be if I let one of them lazy bums stay here without me cracking the whip on him, yes?"

Gilchrist described how he'd painted the concrete steps using an oil-based marine enamel. ("Costs more, but wears four times longer.") Each floor contained two flights and a landing in between. Working efficiently, the painter had finished the flight down to the third floor, its landing and almost down to the first floor landing before breaking for lunch at eleven-thirty.

Lunch had stretched to an extra beer and one o'clock.

"What the hell?" grinned Mr. Gilchrist, his teeth flashing as he repositioned his white canvas painter's cap. "I'm my own boss, yes?"

"But when I finally got back to the paintbrushes, bless Jesus if somebody hadn't walked right down through my whole morning's work!"

In all the time he and his crew had moved up and down the stairwell, they had never once met any tenants there.

"Me, I got careless," Gilchrist admitted. "Didn't seem like there was any need to stick up signs all over the place. My own fault, yes?"

He had backtracked up to the landing between the third and second floors where the morning's paint was still so wet that it didn't take many brush strokes to undo the damage, figuring he'd come back the next day after the higher steps and dried completely so he could paint over the footprints. The longer he worked, though, the more he'd worried.

"I got to thinking what if the guy was wearing expensive treads or threads. He could set me back plenty in a small claims court, yes?"

At last, he'd gone down to speak to the doorman and that was when he first learned of the murder. ("No, don't think I ever saw the lady and they say she was one you remembered, yes?") He'd hung around awhile, listened to the talk and speculations and when the tentative estimates about time of the murder began, he'd started wondering where those hasty footprints originated.

"And?" asked Sigrid.

"That's right, Lieutenant," Gilchrist said. "Right out that door, just as plain as applesauce."

"Looks like a man's size seven boot, Lieutenant," said the lab technician, who'd hoped to end his shift on time this afternoon. From the size of the shoe print and length of stride, they would be able to theorize about the man's height. Paint samples were taken in case the shoes in question turned up, and exhaustive photographs were also taken; but there was nothing distinctive about the foot-

prints, nothing so useful as trademarks or ridged rubber
soles, though Tillie made a quick sketch of the shape of
the boot heel.

"Just in case," he told Sigrid sheepishly.

Mr. Gilchrist was thanked and asked to leave the stairwell untouched for the time being. Sigrid released the rest
of the lab men and she and Tillie returned to apartment 3-
D where Officer Crowell's ears were still being blasted by
authentic rock tapes.

"Doesn't seem to be anything here but music, ma'am"
he reported regretfully as they re-entered the living room.

He was told that all detecting was not as exciting or as
simple as picking up a telephone and discovering a wiretap.
He was told to keep listening and Sigrid and Tillie walked
down to the kitchen looking for some quiet in which to
compare notes.

Even though the sun had long since moved to the other
side of the building, the kitchen still seemed sunlit. The
cabinets were painted buttercup yellow and the countertops
were white formica, but there was no clutter on the
counters. No mushroom-shaped salt and pepper shakers
or clever napkin holders, no cannisters or cookie jar, no
appliances visible at all except the coffee maker, which had
been in active use.

Had it not been for the splashy yellow and orange floral
wall covering, the room could have doubled as a testing
laboratory. Flowers and bright colors yet, like the whole
apartment, stripped down to the bare efficiency.

Sigrid wondered what that said about Julie Redmond's
character? Everything or nothing?

The round white breakfast table was molded in one piece
of plastic, with a central pedestal for support, and Sigrid
drew up a chair and spread out her notes. Although she
and Tillie had avoided stepping on it, neither was unduly
bothered by the chalked outline on the orange-tiled floor.
(I'm getting hard, Sigrid thought sadly.)

The coffee maker was still plugged in, so Tillie located
cups and spoons to pour them each some of the now bitter
brew and they discussed what they had so far.

"The doorman, a Samuel Dorritt, confirmed what Mr.

and Mrs. Cavatori told us," Tillie began. "He says he got a cab for her and the little boy about ten-thirty and another for the ex-husband around eleven."

"How secure is this building?"

"Not very. Dorritt's supposed to know everyone coming in or out, and it's pretty tight at night; but during the day, when he's on duty, the doors are unlocked and sometimes he has to go up to the avenue to hail a cab—something he does for the good tippers like the Cavatoris, so I suppose anyone could walk in then."

"Get someone to check out the cab Redmond took. Make sure he didn't double back."

Tillie made a note of it and added, "It fits in with what the Cavatori maids told me." He showed Sigrid the rough timetable he'd begun:

    10:15—Mrs. Cavatori to Redmond apartment, 3-D
    10:20—Karl Redmond to visit Vico Cavatori, 3-B
    10:29—Mrs. C. and Timmy Redmond leave 3-D
    11:00—Redmond leaves 3-B (Mr. C. sees him enter
        elevator, Dorritt sees him leave.)
    11:15—Mr. C. leaves 3-B
    11:30–1:00—Someone leaves 3rd floor by service
        stairs
    1:15—Body discovered by Miss Fitzpatrick from 3-C

"Somewhere you need to add what Miss Fitzpatrick told me," said Sigrid. "She overheard Julie Redmond speaking to someone angrily in what Miss Fitzpatrick refers to as midmorning. She couldn't be any more specific than that; but if it's any help, she eats breakfast at six-thirty."

Tillie grinned at the faint shudder in Sigrid's tone. Her aversion to early morning hours had indicated to him the first chink in the lieutenant's protective armor.

"Could that be our unknown who took the stairs?"

"Possibly. Miss Fitzpatrick only heard the girl's voice." Sigrid referred to her own sketchy notes. "'He's mine and you can damn well stay away from him' is what she said she heard."

"Talking to another woman? Maybe about that George she made the tape on?"

"Or to her ex-husband about the boy?" Sigrid suggested. She tapped her pencil on Tillie's timetable. "Everyone keeps saying around eleven. That could be a six- or eight-minute spread, you know. Quite sufficient time. Can we be sure Redmond came straight down after Mr. Cavatori saw him into the elevator?"

"I'll check it," Tillie said. "And I'll also see what Records has on the brother, Mickey Novak."

They had found an address book by the bedside telephone and Sigrid riffled through its pages. Julie Redmond's efficiency seemed to have carried over to her personal records, she noted: Names were entered in ink, but addresses and telephone numbers were lightly penciled in a clear and curiously childish handwriting.

The space under Karl Redmond's name was slightly rough, as if more than one address had been erased since the book was begun. Sigrid recognized the current address as somewhere in lower Manhattan.

The rest of the listings included three Georges but nothing to indicate which, if any, was the George of the telephone tap. She slid the book across the shiny white table top to Tillie.

"When you get back to the office, have someone start running a check on these names. See if you can winnow out the right George. I'll take Karl Redmond myself."

As she divided immediate chores and mapped out the routine, Sigrid became aware of voices out in the vestibule. From her seat in the kitchen, she could see down the narrow hallway through the open service door to where one of Officer Crowell's colleagues from the precinct stood guard duty. He was speaking to a tall, cadaverous-looking man and seemed annoyed by the older man's badgering.

"—you don't like it, talk to the Lieutenant," they heard him say.

Tillie got up and walked down to the door. "Something wrong, Mr. Dorritt?"

The man glared at Tillie truculently. "How much longer? Respectable building here."

"Where a woman's just been murdered," Tillie reminded him mildly. "And only this morning, too. You can't expect us to be finished so quickly."

"Is that the doorman?" Sigrid called. Although he was informally clothed now, his build and the way he carried his head reminded her that she'd seen him in the living room when she'd first arrived. "Ask him to come in, please."

Dorritt was a tall, almost gaunt figure. He had rounded shoulders and his head bobbled forward on a long scrawny neck, making him look somewhat like a thin, elderly turtle. His eyes were deep-set and his iron gray hair was closely trimmed and combed flat. He wore uniform pants with a dark red stripe down the side, but instead of doorman's jacket, his pants were topped by an open-necked white shirt and an old maroon cardigan which had been clumsily darned at the elbows. On his wrinkled face was a mulish look of suspicion mingled with stubbornness.

Tillie introduced Sigrid and said, "You told me before, Mr. Dorritt, that you were in the lobby when Karl Redmond came down in the elevator. Then Vico Cavatori came down about ten minutes later. Are you sure it wasn't the other way around?"

Dorritt's head swung around the bright yellow and orange kitchen, bobbled in Sigrid's direction, then back to Tillie.

"Wasn't there," he said.

"But you distinctly told me—" Tillie began indignantly.

"Wasn't me." Malicious humor briefly sparked the old man's pale blue eyes. "My brother."

At Tillie's unbelieving stare, he shrugged his thin shoulders indifferently. "Twins. Identical. He's Sammy. I'm Manny."

Sigrid gazed at him, bemused, trying to picture the proud delight this tall bony man and his brother must have excited in a mother's heart over sixty years ago. Samuel and Emanuel.

Imagination turned somersaults with the vision, was firmly restrained.

"Do both of you work here?" she asked.

Manny Dorritt rationed out his words as reluctantly as a miser spending gold, but he nodded and grudgingly volunteered that he and his twin, who was working the day shift this week and to whom Tillie had spoken earlier, not only shared the doorman's job but also the doorman's single uniform jacket and gold-braided hat. ("Stingy owners," said Dorritt, without rancor.) There was no full-time resident janitor. Regular cleaning and repairs of the building were performed by a maintenance service, but the Dorritt brothers had been given the use of a small basement apartment in return for minor janitorial duties involving fuses and thermostats and cut-off valves.

The brothers worked two shifts: from seven to four in the afternoon and from four to midnight, the off-duty one spelling the other at lunch and supper time. That meant that Manny Dorritt had been in the lobby from around twelve till one P.M. and had missed both the comings and goings of the third-floor tenants as well as Miss Fitzpatrick's discovery of Julie Redmond's body.

"So during the hour you were on duty, no one went up to the third floor?" asked Sigrid.

Dorritt's pendulous head swung around to her again. "Busy time. Doors to open. Packages to hold. Didn't watch to see what floors the cage stopped at."

He pursed his thin, liverish lips as if so much garrulity pained him. Sigrid waited, gazing at him with her calm gray eyes. Tillie recognized her tactic and didn't interrupt.

Dorritt turned his head from one to the other uneasily. The silence grew, and up from the dim recesses of Manny Dorritt's memory floated the image of a fourth-grade teacher who had never been fooled as to which particular Dorritt twin had committed which infraction of the rules. She'd had gray eyes, too. Eyes that bored into you until you couldn't help coming out with the truth. Dorritt's rounded shoulders slumped in capitulation.

"Saw her brother," he said sullenly. "Just after twelve. Didn't see me."

He'd been a couple of minutes late relieving Sammy for lunch, he explained in monosyllables, so Sammy had already gone downstairs, leaving the doorman's jacket and hat inside their little cubbyhole just off the lobby. He'd entered the lobby from the street a pace or two behind the dead woman's brother.

"Mickey Novak?" asked Tillie.

Dorritt nodded. He described the small, dark-haired young man whom he'd known by sight as wearing white denim jeans and jacket and a green shirt. Without his own distinctive hat and elaborate doorman's jacket, he hadn't been recognized by Novak.

"None of 'em do. They see you on the street like this, they pass you up," the doorman said bitterly. The old grievance made him almost loquacious. "Think they're being so gawdamighty friendly when you're holding the door or getting 'em a cab. Not to you. To the frigging uniform."

By persistent questioning, they learned that Mickey Novak had passed through the lobby and into the elevator at a minute or two past twelve, but the noon hour was the busiest time of day and if Dorritt had seen Julie Redmond's brother depart, he wasn't admitting it.

Sigrid rather suspected there was something else Dorritt wasn't telling, but she thanked him for his cooperation and indicated that they had no more questions for the moment. "We should be finished for the day shortly ourselves," she told him.

Dorritt started to leave, then turned back. "Taking him with you?" he asked, his head bobbing toward the patrolman at the end of the service hall.

Tillie explained that an officer would be on watch there until they were completely finished with the Redmond apartment, which might take another day or two. Dorritt started to argue, thought better of it, and reluctantly departed.

A disappointed Officer Frederick Crowell appeared to report that no taped conversations had been masquerading as rock tapes. He, too, was thanked and sent back to his precinct station.

Tillie looked longingly at the ransacked desk. His methodical soul was drawn by muddled papers in need of sorting and cataloguing, but Sigrid dissuaded him. "They'll wait till tomorrow," she said. "First things first."

He nodded, called the local precinct to confirm a routine round-the-clock watch outside apartment 3-D and collected the dead girl's address book to take back to headquarters.

"Unless you want me to come with you to see Redmond?" he asked.

"Not necessary," she said.

Out in the vestibule, she hesitated before Miss Fitzpatrick's door, then decided to tackle young Eliza at a later time.

The lone police officer stood alertly as they locked the two doors and prepared to leave, but he was an old hand at long stretches of guard duty and had already secured a fairly comfortable arm chair which he'd positioned just inside the small recess formed by the corner of the enclosed stairwell near 3-D's service door.

The elevator stopped with a soft chime and as soon as the door closed upon his superiors, he loosened his collar and settled back for an easy, if boring, evening.

CHAPTER 7

It was still daylight when Sigrid parked her car near Father Fagan Square and walked up MacDougal Street through a diversity of people and wares crowding the sidewalks. Bursts of Chinese, Spanish, and Italian were heard as frequently as English along these SoHo streets.

Among its dingier neighbors, Number 2 Princess Alley reminded Sigrid of Dickens's Mrs. Cratchit, brave in ribbons. The front of the old two-story brick building glistened in shiny green enamel; the windows were bedizened with spangles and glitter, and above them, the name *Brummagems* had been painted in a flowing gold script which owed more to verve than expertise.

As Sigrid entered the shop, a delicate tinkle made her glance up. The doorbell was a white stained-glass lily with petals gracefully turned back from dainty pistils tipped by a cluster of minute brass bells, each no bigger than the end of a hatpin. They tinkled again when she closed the door and from the rear of the shop, Sigrid heard a voice call, "With you in a minute."

She gazed around with mildly curious eyes. Jewelry did

not interest her much. The few pieces she owned were modest keepsakes: an old ruby ring from Grandmother Lattimore that had been in the family for five generations, an oval pin of seed pearls, a handful of silver bracelets her mother had once sent from a bazaar in Marrakech, a child's gold locket which had been bought for another Sigrid over a hundred years ago in Copenhagen.

The trendy things in this shop were light years away in feeling. In the center of the store, a hexagonal column had been covered with line drawings of angular exotic faces. Large organdy ears jutted from the faces and each lobe was pierced by earrings fashioned from colored glass, polished rocks, sea shells, chunks of wood, feathers, and a dozen different materials. Wooden hands protruded regally from one wall and every wooden finger and wrist were similarly adorned.

On the opposite wall, serried ranks of Styrofoam wig stands had been sprayed a matte black to dramatize neck- laces of shiny wood and chunky beads. A similarly painted window dresser's dummy stood by the high rear counter, immodestly clad only in belts fashioned of plastic and chrome blocks. The mannequin's head was inclined toward the silent blond girl behind the counter who bent over a workbench cluttered with bits and pieces of all the things displayed in the shop.

The girl looked up and smiled. "Only a minute more," she promised.

She held up a square of Lucite so polished that its beveled edges looked like cut glass. It was about an inch square and embedded within its crystal clarity was an intricate design in burnished brass wire that began as a link in a chain outside the plastic and, after completing a labyrin- thian pattern, exited on the opposite side into another link.

"It's my new design for a necklace," said the girl. "How are you going to like it?"

"Very much," Sigrid said and was faintly surprised to realize that she truly did.

"Of course, it really ought to be gold," sighed the girl. "Brass just won't hold that shine. But electroplate's not much better."

She was pure Flemish, thought Sigrid, who favored late Gothic drawings. The girl had a plain, ethereal beauty like one of those Holbein silverpoints—a thin face with high clear forehead and hair so fair as to be almost white. Not exactly pretty, but so self-contained that she radiated serenity.

She wore a loosely draped peasant-style dress of unbleached muslin that made the analogy to Flemish angels not too unlikely. Then she stood up and walked around the counter and Sigrid caught her breath.

No, not angel but madonna. The girl was in the very last stages of pregnancy.

"Did you have anything special in mind?"

"Is Karl Redmond here?" Sigrid asked.

The girl shook her head. "No. May I help you instead?"

"I'm Lieutenant Harald, Police Department," Sigrid explained, holding out her shield and watching the girl's face closely.

There was no apprehension, only professional interest as she reached for Sigrid's gleaming shield. "May I?" she asked and held it up to the light to scrutinize the engraving.

"That's really not very clean work," she said disapprovingly as she handed it back. "The lettering could be much sharper. I suppose you're here because of Julie?"

"You know that she's been killed, Mrs.—?"

"Bryna Leighton, but it's Miss, not Mrs.," the girl corrected. "Luisa Cavatori called Karl late this afternoon to tell him. And then Karl left to discuss a business deal with Mr. Cavatori's partner."

"About the zipper pulls?"

"How did you know?"

"I was there when Mr. Cavatori showed one to his wife and said that Mr. Redmond had tried to interest him in them."

The girl's vague air sharpened into interest. "What did he say? Did he like them? Did she?"

Before Sigrid could answer, the girl seemed to stiffen for an instant. She looked at the clock behind her, frowned, then turned back to her work bench to jot the time on a notepad.

"The pains are coming pretty regularly," she said. "Do you think I ought to call the midwife yet?"

In the next moment, the question became rhetorical as a severe contraction doubled her over.

"My car's not far," Sigrid said hastily. "I can have you at a hospital in no time. I have a siren," she added inanely.

"Hospital?" said Bryna Leighton. "Oh no. We're having the baby here."

Sigrid looked around wildly. Nowhere did she see a suitable birthing area. She took a deep breath. She would stay completely calm, she told herself. She would remember the compulsory first-aid course she'd had as a rookie. Among other things, it had included obstetrics instructions.

Hadn't it?

She tried to remember and found her mind going blank.

"I think," said Bryna, "that I'd better go upstairs. Would you call Mrs. Li for me? She's my midwife. The number's there by the phone."

She paused at the doorway to the stairs. "Tell her the contractions are coming every five minutes now."

Sigrid dived for the telephone, dialed, and was answered in a spate of Chinese. "Mrs. Li," she enunciated carefully. "Please let me speak to Mrs. Li."

There was a confused murmur at the other end of the wire, then an adolescent male voice said, "Mom's not here, but we expect her any minute. Want me to have her call you?"

"One of her clients is having a baby," Sigrid said. "Right now."

She gave him Bryna's name and address. "Tell her the contractions are coming every five minutes."

"Hang on a second," said the boy. There was a pause, then he returned. "My grandmother says for you not to worry. This is Bryna's first, so there's lots of time."

A midwife's mother would certainly know what she was talking about, Sigrid assured herself, and she followed the stairs up to the large, cheerfully messy loft, relayed the grandmother's encouraging words, and was dismayed to see Bryna shake her head doubtfully.

"The books say an average first baby takes five to twelve hours, but I think mine's going to be quicker. Anyhow, I've been having regular contractions all afternoon."

Sigrid was appalled. "And you didn't call anybody?"

"I thought it might be false labor. The baby's not due for another week."

She had stripped the couch-bed, covered the mattress with plastic and was trying to tuck in a fresh bottom sheet when another contraction hit her. "Jot the time on that pad," she gasped.

Sigrid scanned the previous figures. "Every *four* minutes?" she asked nervously.

She seemed to recall from that long-ago training film that the tempo really picked up once the pains were down to five minutes apart.

"Maybe if you'd lie down that would slow things. I can finish making the bed with you in it."

Bryna looked around. "There's so much I should do," she said.

"*I'll* do it," said Sigrid. "Will you *please*—lie—*down!*"

Bryna giggled. "According to all the stereotypes, only the fathers flip out. Women are supposed to be cool and efficient. Besides, aren't you people trained to help in emergency births, like cab drivers?"

"I've never seen a baby born," Sigrid said tightly. "I've heard the theory, but I've never had any practice."

She bundled up the used linens and found a hamper to deposit them in.

Bryna changed into a simple short gown and eased herself into bed. "Janey Li will probably get here in plenty of time," she comforted Sigrid.

Another contraction washed over her.

"On the other hand," she said, when it had subsided, "maybe we'd better be prepared. The pads are in that blue dry cleaner's bag under the dresser."

The sack was heavier than it looked.

"Each pad's a folded section of the *Times* stitched into an old pillow case," Bryna explained. "They're to soak up the blood."

Sigrid turned white and occupied herself with clearing

off the dining table, stacking the day's accumulation of dirty dishes in the sink, and, at Bryna's suggestion, scouring out her largest pot, which she filled with water and set on the gas stove to start heating.

By then, day had waned to twilight. Sigrid switched on extra lamps as she moved around the loft straightening and tidying away some of the clutter.

"You're compulsively neat, aren't you?" asked the girl. She lay propped on a couple of pillows and watched Sigrid's efforts as if it were totally natural that a police officer should do maid service. "Let the rest go. Come talk to me. Are you married?"

"No."

"Why not?"

"Why aren't you?" asked Sigrid tartly.

"Touché. My family thinks I'm trying to prove something. That I'm the new woman, totally liberated." She shrugged. "The truth is, I can't forget I'm Catholic."

Her hands rested lightly on her swollen belly and she patted it ruefully. "I know that sounds silly. Technically, I'm living in sin and my baby will be a bastard, but a civil ceremony wouldn't change anything. Even though I don't go to church as often as I should, I still believe its teachings and there's no way around it: Marriage is a sacrament and Karl's still married to Julie in the eyes of the church."

She hesitated. "*Was* married," she amended in a small voice. "I wish he'd come home. We went to all those natural childbirth classes together, but he paid more attention. I don't know if I'm supposed to be deep-breathing or panting. Do you suppose I'm second stage yet?"

"Oh, surely not," Sigrid said, wondering just how many stages there were. She darkly suspected there might be only two. "Where's that midwife?"

"Don't worry—what did you say your name was?"

"Lieutenant Harald."

"No, I mean your first name. Look, in about twenty minutes, if Karl and Janey don't get here, I'm probably going to be clawing the walls. I really doubt that I can yell Lieutenant Harald every time the pain hits, so can't we drop some of the formality?"

"My name is Sigrid," she said stiffly.

"Nice to meet you, Sigrid. I'm Bryna." The girl spoke lightly, but a fine line of perspiration glinted along her upper lip.

Sigrid brought a cool cloth for her face and brushed the silver-blond hair back from her high forehead. Training told her that she should be using the girl's lowered guard to question her about Karl's relation with his ex-wife, but a sense of fairness prevented her. Not now, not like this.

"Did you see Julie's body?" Bryna asked between long, deliberate breaths.

"Yes."

"Funny, isn't it? The way she affected our life and yet I never once saw her. Not even a picture. She was beautiful though, wasn't she?"

"Yes."

"They say Timmy looks just like her. I don't know. And Karl doesn't say. But maybe that's why he and Timmy don't—"

She broke off abruptly. "You don't talk much, do you, Sigrid? And I'm babbling. Sorry. This isn't your usual social situation, is it? Karl wanted so badly for us to be married before the baby came. It's the only thing we ever fight about. He *hates* thinking that I feel he's still married to Julie. I tried to explain that it wasn't me really, but the church.

"I guess there's a lot of paperwork involved in getting a baby legitimized. Now that Julie's dead, we could drag Father Ambrose in to marry us right now and everything'd be as proper as white gloves, and yet Karl's just as much its father now as he'll be next week. Silly technicalities. *Uh-oh!*"

She clasped Sigrid's hand so tightly that Sigrid winced, and Bryna's steady, deliberately deep breaths became shallow and rapid.

"Get some towels!" she panted.

Sigrid rushed to the bathroom, scooped up an armload from the shelf behind the door and rushed back. "What's happened?" she cried.

"My water just broke and I'm sopping!"

"I'll do that," said a new voice, and Sigrid whirled around to see a pleasant-faced Chinese-American woman who'd entered unnoticed in the emergency.

"Trying to have this baby without me, Bryna?" she teased. She slipped the towels under Bryna's hips, then opened her satchel.

"Oh, Janey, I thought you'd never get here!"

Sigrid had not really expected a wizened Oriental with pigtail and Mao jacket, but Janey Li's youth surprised her. She looked barely twenty and was dressed in crisp white, as befitted someone who was not only a trained midwife but also a registered nurse. To Sigrid's infinite relief, Mrs. Li also looked beautifully efficient and Sigrid was quite willing to stand aside and let her get on with it.

In the next instant she wasn't even needed as a strong hand to hold onto. Karl Redmond came racing up the stairs, out of breath. From three blocks away, he'd seen Mrs. Li enter their shop and had run as fast as he could. Tie askew, he slid into Sigrid's chair and clasped Bryna's hand.

"Pant-pant-blow, darling!" he said, panting himself. "Pant-pant-blow."

Neither he nor Mrs. Li seemed to question her presence and Bryna was too occupied to remember anything so prosaic as introductions. She was bearing down now, all her concentration centered on birthing her baby.

"Bring another lamp," Mrs. Li called, and Sigrid meekly did as she was told.

While fetching and emptying basins of hot water, she heard Karl Redmond say, "We've got a contract, darling! That's what took me so long. Once Fuselli saw our samples, he wanted the papers drawn up right then. I got Pop's old lawyer to come over. He said the terms aren't just fair, they could have been written by my fairy godmother. And Vico's going to guarantee the loan we need. We could start tooling a production line tomorrow!"

"Tomorrow's Sunday," Bryna murmured.

"Then Monday," he said, tenderly wiping her face with a damp cloth Sigrid had handed him. "Right after we get a marriage license."

"Stop talking and push!" said Mrs. Li.

Bryna bore down hard and waves of pain rippled through

her body as she pushed again and yet again. From her post
directly behind the midwife, Sigrid saw the baby's head
emerge, followed by tiny shoulders and then with a gush
of bloody liquid, the rest of the body, entangled in the
sinuous cord.

Almost immediately, and without any help from Janey
Li, came the thin, unmistakable newborn crying.

Sigrid was transfixed and could not tear her eyes away,
repelled and fascinated simultaneously. As part of her police training, she had seen films of childbirth, but the reality
was both easier and bloodier than she'd envisioned. The
umbilical cord was thicker, too, like a living flesh-and-
blood cable.

Half her mind tried to record Janey Li's actions in case
this situation ever arose again, but the other half of her was
strangely moved, remembering an old line of Latin, *Inter
urina et faeces nascent sum*—between urine and feces are we
born.

And what could have been disgusting was instead tran-
scendently beautiful.

Bryna's fair hair was matted with sweat, but her smile
was radiant when Janey Li laid the newborn infant, loosely
wrapped in a cotton flannel blanket and still wailing, across
her abdomen and said, "Here she is, kids!"

During the last few minutes, Sigrid had been vaguely
conscious of voices and movements in the shadows across
the room by the doorway leading to the stairs. At Janey
Li's words, a voice cried, "It's a girl!" and a noisy cheer
went up.

Six or eight young men and women spilled into the loft.
There was a pop of champagne corks and a clink of glasses
as the baby's arrival was toasted by her parents' friends.

Sigrid was not so much shunted aside as gently pre-
empted by young women who seemed to have done this
before. Soon, Janey Li had finished her work and mother
and baby were carefully sponged clean. Afterbirth and
bloody linens were whisked away, fresh sheets and pillow-
cases appeared, and someone had brought an armful of
daisies, enough to fill a dozen jars and vases around the
big room.

A wiry youth had begun washing dishes at the sink and

a tall bearded man handed Sigrid and Mrs. Li water glasses abrim with amber effervescence. Hushed happiness ringed the bed where Bryna and her infant lay in drowsy exhaustion, but laughter and euphoria enveloped Karl Redmond's side of the loft.

Silence fell completely when a young black girl, slim and straight as a hunting spear, detached herself from the group, and, with ritualistic formality, approached the foot of Bryna's bed.

Behind her, two musicians began weaving a net of poignant harmony with wooden flutes.

"What is thy daughter to be called?" she asked. Her English was overlaid with an unfamiliar accent.

"Her name is Katrina," said Bryna with matching solemnity.

"Katrina," said the girl, "thou art welcome among us."

Her voice rose in clear liquid notes and the flutes twined in and around African words Sigrid could not understand.

"It's a welcoming song the women of her tribe sing to greet a newborn," whispered Janey Li.

Half Gregorian chant, half Dorian mode, the song's tones shifted like the colors of a taffeta gown in firelight and the wooden flutes dodged behind and above in subtle counterpoint. Bryna smiled at Karl, who bent to touch their sleeping daughter's tiny face; and a sudden tightness constricted Sigrid's throat.

Perhaps it was knowing what the song signified, perhaps it was the simple, uncomplicated friendship between the people here. Or maybe it was only the champagne.

Whatever the reason, there was such an unbearable sweetness to the scene that Sigrid knew she would remember this spring night forever.

Blindly, she set her glass on the nearest table and slipped from the loft unnoticed.

CHAPTER 8

On the third floor of the Rensselaer Building, Officer Hodson cocked an alert eye as the elevator doors slid open again upon the gaunt frame of one of the Dorritt brothers. Which Dorritt would be hard to say. Like Detective Tildon and Lieutenant Harald earlier, Hodson had been startled to realize that there were two identically tall and elderly doormen.

"Yeah?" he asked, for this was the second time a Dorritt had come up tonight.

The man's gloomy eyes inspected the vestibule's molding. "Thought you might be hungry," he said. "Thought I'd watch for you if you want to go eat." His head swung round and bobbled sourly at the policeman.

"Thanks," said Hodson, "but somebody'll be bringing me a sandwich around nine."

"Humph!" said Dorritt. He glared at Hodson with those deep-set eyes, then shuffled back into the elevator and was gone without further speech.

Not exactly the most gracious offer he'd ever received, thought Hodson, returning to his newspaper.

• • •

When Sigrid unlocked her door shortly after nine that evening, the steady tap-tapping of a tack hammer from the depths of her apartment warned that she might not be able to head for a hot tub as directly as she'd planned.

"Roman?" she called.

"Don't look!" answered a deep male voice and a door at the end of the hall banged shut.

On the cookie-cutter grid in the rental agent's office, Sigrid's high-rise apartment was designated a two-bedroom model; but she used the minuscule space of that second bedroom as a catchall for the small amount of clutter she allowed in her life.

At the moment, the room was dominated by an enormous old chair she'd salvaged off the sidewalk last month. Until then, all her furniture had been legitimately purchased from proper department stores and she'd never quite understood what was meant when enthusiasts spoke of character in a chest or table. And certainly she'd never been tempted to scavenge anybody's castoffs.

But then she'd stumbled across the chair parked next to a cluster of garbage cans, awaiting the city trash-removal truck with dignified patience, and she'd succumbed to its massive grotesqueries. It was over five feet tall, the two uprights at the back terminating in a pair of snarling lions' heads as large as a house cat's. The broad armrests also ended in the hand-carved heads and clear green agates were embedded in the eye sockets.

Sigrid had stripped away the cracked brown leather and begun scraping down the wood before being plagued by serious doubts about the way the chair was going to look if she ever got it finished. It certainly wouldn't match anything in the rest of her apartment. She had repeated her doubts to Roman Tramegra, who came, looked, and immediately co-opted the project for his own.

"I'll take step-by-step photographs and write an illustrated article on reupholstering for *Flea Market Living*," he announced. "They only pay two cents a word, but it's twenty dollars for every picture." He optimistically estimated that he could stretch the work for at least a dozen 35mm color slides.

Without planning to, Sigrid found herself handing over her extra latchkey so that Tramegra could come and go freely. So far, the arrangement was working better than she'd expected. He seemed hesitant to impinge on her privacy and was usually gone before she returned; yet once or twice, she'd come home to find that he'd cooked dinner—enough for both of them, although he always had to be urged to stay.

Tonight appeared to be such an occasion. There was an unfamiliar odor emanating from the kitchen, a faintly charred smell of something which had been browned not wisely but too well. Roman Tramegra was an inventive cook. Not all his inventions were divinely inspired.

"Ah, there you are!" he said, pulling the door shut behind him. As the chair neared completion, he had put the room off limits until the final unveiling. "I was hoping you'd get home before the broccoli casserole completely dried out."

Roman Tramegra was another of her mother's impulsive good deeds. Anne Harald was an award-winning photojournalist and, while on a magazine assignment in Italy, she'd run across Tramegra in rather distressing circumstances. She'd encouraged him to return to the States and had even lent him her vacant apartment while he sorted things out again.

He was a large, soft man of indeterminate middle age, rather like a well-pampered Persian cat. His light sandy hair was brushed forward over a fast-receding hairline and his soft brown eyes were hooded; yet, like even the most sedentary cat's, they were watchful eyes, and Sigrid knew that if she showed the slightest distaste for his casserole or his company, he would take himself off, feelings bruised perhaps, but without reproach.

"Broccoli casserole?" she asked, trying to sound positive. "I hope you made enough for both of us."

"Why thank you, my dear, I think it'll stretch. I used a base of mushroom soup," he explained happily, "a layer of broccoli, four diced frankfurters and then a can of tomato soup with just a pinch of parsley from your new terrarium."

"Terrarium? Roman, I don't have a terrarium."

A sense of foreboding touched her. "You don't mean that big jar I left on the counter, do you?"

Tramegra was stricken. "Were you saving the parsley for something special?" he asked. "Really, I only took the teensiest bit, but I'll go up to the avenue right now and buy you some more if I didn't leave enough."

"It's not that," she assured him, heading for the kitchen. "I just hope you washed it thoroughly."

Tramegra trailed after her. "Washed?" he said. "Well, of *course* I did. At least I rinsed it under the tap. I mean, how dirty could it be growing in that jar? Oh dear! It wasn't *poison*, was it? I was so certain it was parsley. I never thought about hemlock or nightshade!"

Upon meeting Sigrid, Tramegra had instantly decided to write a murder thriller and kept hoping she would give him authentic details which would inspire a bestseller. So far, he'd been disappointed by what she'd let drop of her day-to-day cases. Did she never handle anything exotic? Something with blow darts or tarantulas? "Guns are commonplace, and blunt instruments are so tacky," he kept complaining.

Now he was excited by the possibility that she'd finally relented, had actually brought home a poisonous plant that he could use in a story.

"It was only parsley," said Sigrid, deflating his hopes. "But there were caterpillars on it. Swallowtail butterfly larvae."

She took a magnifying glass from a pencil jar on the counter and examined the clump of parsley which remained inside the jar. Three hairy little worms still munched away with single-minded devotion. She tried to remember just how many Jill Gill had given her. Three seemed about right, but she'd certainly examine each forkful of any broccoli casserole Roman served her, just in case.

As might have been predicted, Tramegra's magpie attention was diverted by the caterpillars.

Sigrid was unclear about his finances, but she suspected

that a small income from some unknown source paid for necessities. For the extravagances of his life, he sold bits and scraps of freelance writing to magazines, newspapers and trade journals. Tramegra's markets, like *Flea Market Living,* were seldom the high-paying slick magazines, but this never discouraged him.

Under his enthusiastic questions, Sigrid relayed everything Dr. Gill had told her about the different life stages of this particular butterfly and was amused to see Roman's interest turn calculating.

"It's a natural for *Jack and Jill* or *Humpty Dumpty,*" he said. "Or—with some really sharp pictures—*Ranger Rick.* Tie in the scientific and environmental aspect. I shall call it 'City Pets for City Kids.'"

"They eat parsley, celery tops, and dill," said Sigrid, more than willing to delegate their care to someone else. Nauman was quite mistaken if he thought she yearned for small, fuzzy creatures to coo over.

She glanced at the time and realized that he must be far out over the Atlantic by now. And she didn't miss him at all, she told herself, as she watched Roman dish out the broccoli casserole.

CHAPTER 9

The night was a mixed success for Eliza Fitzpatrick. As she'd guessed (and hoped), Aunt Elizabeth refused to listen to reason and would not allow herself to be dislodged.

Gilbert Fitzpatrick presented cogent legalistic arguments; but Aunt Elizabeth remained adamant and, in Eliza's view, her logic was impeccable: Julie Redmond's killer had accomplished what he desired and had departed unobserved. Lack of witnesses and the open door were proof that he had not been disturbed or hurried, so there was little reason to suppose that he would return. And even if he did, continued Aunt Elizabeth, why would he bother with her? Indeed, how could he, when a policeman had been left there on guard?

"But you shouldn't be alone now," Fitzpatrick had argued. "You have taken a sedative and if you should fall—"

"I am much more likely to fall in *your* home than in my own," Aunt Elizabeth had said crisply. Her apartment might look like an overcrowded antique store, but every footstool and hand-hooked scatter rug occupied a familiar spot and she could thread her way through the maze blind-folded if need be.

Her nephew conceded that the same could not be said for his home.

"I'll stay over, if you like," Eliza volunteered.

Her father looked at her suspiciously.

"I can finish reading *Wuthering Heights* here just as well as at home," Eliza said, rummaging in her book bag for note cards and trying to appear indifferent as to whether or not she'd be allowed to spend the night next door to a real murder scene.

Her air was convincing and he had finally departed for the night, fussily making sure that the door was double-locked behind him.

Her mother, more perceptive, had rung up a half hour later. "I want your word of honor that you won't go chasing all over that building tonight," she said.

"Oh, Mom!"

"Don't 'Oh, Mom' me," said maternal authority. "I don't know what you thought you'd be missing if you didn't stay there tonight, but you're not to poke your nose into things that don't concern you. I mean it, Eliza."

"I was just trying to be helpful," said Eliza, injured.

"So long as you limit your helpfulness to Aunt Eliza-beth," her mother replied. "I knew it was a mistake to let you read all those Nancy Drew books."

Eliza laughed and hung up the phone.

Until ten o'clock, when Aunt Elizabeth finally toddled off to bed, she had been the dutiful, studious niece; had, in truth, finished reading *Wuthering Heights* and jotted down the main points she wanted to make in her paper about repressed sexuality and the status of women in the nineteenth century. But with Aunt Elizabeth safely tucked away, she had tiptoed down to the front door and peered through the fisheye peephole that provided a good view of the vestibule from the elevator on the left to the stairwell doors opposite.

Beyond the corner of the stairwell, she could just see the edge of Officer Hodson's blue bulk as he sat absorbed in an evening newspaper.

Without a single qualm—five or ten feet from Aunt Elizabeth's threshold hardly constituted chasing all over the building, she rationalized—Eliza opened the door and gave Hodson a friendly smile.

"Doesn't it get lonely being on guard all night?" she asked.

The silent building, the vestibule's indirect lighting, the lateness of the hour—all were conducive to introspective conversation. Eliza planned to study law herself; and with her budding lawyer's skill, it took her only ten minutes to lead Officer Hodson from a philosophic discussion of routine police work into a general highlighting of some of the more interesting cases he'd worked on. Ten minutes more and they were into the specifics of Julie Redmond's murder, with Hodson pooh-poohing any exotic solutions.

"It'll be the ex-husband or a lover or the lover boy's ex-girlfriend. You'll see."

"How do you know she had a lover?"

"Cupcakes like that've always got a guy on the string," Hodson said flatly.

Eliza started to argue about judging a woman by her looks, but then she recalled that repressed sexuality hadn't exactly been one of Julie's hangups. She conceded the point and sat down on the carpeted floor near him. "Is it always a husband or boyfriend?"

"Or a brother or even a son. At least the ones we solve usually are. Murder's about the most personal crime you can get," he explained, remembering some of the lectures he'd attended at John Jay when he was still trying to make sergeant. "That's what they mean by domestic. It just stands to reason: Who hates you enough to kill you? Somebody who knows you good. And who knows you that good? Your family and your best friends, that's who!"

"And when it's not domestic?" asked Eliza.

"When the killer doesn't know his victim?"

Eliza nodded.

"If we don't nail him in the act, then those are the ones that get dumped in the dead-end files. If they ever get solved, it's usually because a car gets stopped for a license check or the guy gets a speeding ticket. Pure dumb luck, most of the time."

A product of a scientific technological era, Eliza had grown up thinking one could punch the proper data into an electronic keyboard and a precise answer correct to six decimal points would magically appear. She was slightly shocked to realize how easily an impersonal murder could go undetected and hoped that wouldn't be the case here. "Does Lieutenant Harald think it's a boyfriend?" she asked eagerly.

Hodson shrugged, not wanting to admit that a precinct cop was hardly the lieutenant's first sounding board.

"They say she doesn't guess—just waits until she knows. I hear she's got a pretty good batting average," he added generously.

This was what Eliza had really come to hear. Hitching her jeans more comfortably, she drew her knees up together, propped her small pointed chin on them and settled herself to pump Officer Hodson on all he knew about Lieutenant Harald.

"*Eliza!*" exclaimed a scandalized voice. "What on earth are you doing out there alone—unchaperoned!—at this time of night?"

The girl guiltily jumped to her feet.

Without her gold-rimmed glasses, Miss Elizabeth Fitzpatrick looked even tinier than usual, but the tendrils of white curls which sprang around her face did nothing to soften her outraged propriety, and her dignity triumphed even over a pink ruffled nightgown.

"What would your father say if he found you here?"

Eliza sighed and said goodnight to Hodson, who watched her follow a scolding Miss Fitzpatrick back inside 3-C. He regretted the interruption almost as much as Eliza had. Now the evening stretched ahead with nothing to break the monotony.

To give Miss Fitzpatrick her due, she did not belabor Eliza with disapproval once her niece was properly back inside the apartment and pointed toward the bed in the guest room. They said goodnight to each other, then Eliza brushed her teeth and slipped into the oversized football sweatshirt that constituted her nightgown. The sweatshirt—bright red with a gold numeral—struck an incongruous note in the turn-of-the century bedroom.

The spool bed was covered in white dimity spread and dust ruffles and had a matching tester with ruffles and shirrs overhead. It always made Eliza feel like a character in *Little Women*. Unfortunately, the soft, fluffy bed had a surprisingly lumpy mattress and it usually took her half the night to come to terms with it.

Tonight was no different. She kept drifting off to sleep, snuggling deeper into the covers, then coming uncomfortably awake as a leg or arm tried to accommodate an unexpected mound or depression. She thought of Julie and wondered where her body was now.

Among the tenants of the Rensselaer Building, few were given to riotous parties or late nights; and by two, the elevator seemed to have made its last run of the evening. Silence enfolded the building and Officer Hodson had put aside his newspaper and fought his heavy eyelids to a compromise: He would close them, but that certainly didn't mean he was going to sleep.

Within minutes, his lower lip had dropped and his breathing came slower and heavier as he lost his tenuous hold on consciousness.

He was oblivious when someone entered the vestibule almost noiselessly through the stair door and watched him with uneasiness before moving silently away.

At two-thirty Eliza gave up on the lumpy bed and crept down the hall to the kitchen, pausing first by her aunt's door to listen to the faint, ladylike snores. Out in the kitchen, she tried not to rattle the utensils too loudly as she measured cocoa, sugar, and milk into a saucepan. Experience had taught her that only a large mug of hot chocolate would relax her enough to finish the night on that mattress.

Up to this point, she could say with perfect truthfulness that cocoa had been her only reason for getting up. But adding an extra cup of milk to the saucepan bordered on deliberate calculation.

They're guardians of public welfare and safety, she argued silently. Support your local police. Wasn't Dad always saying that citizens weren't properly appreciative? Didn't Aunt Elizabeth believe in charity? How much could it hurt to offer a cup of cocoa to a public servant? She certainly wouldn't stay.

Well . . . she'd only stay long enough for him to drink it so she could bring the cup back. Nobody could complain about that.

All the same, Eliza slipped back down to her room and pulled on her jeans before tiptoeing barefooted to the front door. She'd be in enough trouble if Aunt Elizabeth caught her. Catching her with only a sweatshirt on would probably shock the old darling worse than finding Julie's body.

Grinning at the thought, Eliza pressed her eye to the peephole and was frozen by the scene in the vestibule outside.

At first, it looked as though Officer Hodson had been knocked unconscious by the tall, stooped-shouldered man who stood over him and glared down with clenched fists. Hodson's body seemed loose in the chair, his eyes were closed, and his head drooped to one side. But the stealthy way in which the man moved away made Eliza realize that Hodson was only sleeping. The door was virtually soundproof, but she was willing to bet that there was no jingle as one of the ubiquitous Dorritts separated the passkeys on his ring and fitted one into a lock.

His gaunt, pendulous head turned once more to the sleeping officer before he disappeared inside the apartment.

Eliza gave him time to get well away from the door, then darted across the vestibule and shook Hodson.

He jerked awake, but it was only the girl again, not one of his superiors, thank God! He started to relax when she shook him again and hissed, "It's one of the doormen! He used a passkey to get into that apartment."

"What?" Hodson stood up sharply, his hand automatically unsnapping his holster. Puzzled, he noted the unbroken seals on both doors of the Redmond apartment.

"Not there," whispered the girl. "He went into the Bitzers' apartment." She pointed to 3-A.

"Which door?" Hodson whispered back.

"The main one."

"Okay, you go back inside and close your door," he directed.

Insulted as she felt at being treated like a child, Eliza knew the futility of arguing with bullheaded authority. She retreated to the far side of her aunt's threshold, but kept the door open a tiny crack; and when Hodson tried the door of 3-A, she was watching with her breath held.

The door opened silently at his touch and over his shoulder, Eliza saw that the lights were on inside the entry. Hodson stepped through the door and Eliza followed unnoticed a few feet behind him.

The formal rooms were dark, but as they turned the corner and passed through an opening to the service hall, light could be seen streaming from the kitchen and they heard the clink of glass on porcelain. Suddenly aware of her presence, Hodson glared at her and motioned for her to go back, but Eliza stubbornly held her ground.

Resigned, Hodson rushed forward into the kitchen with his revolver in hand. "Okay, Dorritt!" he cried.

He was drawn up short by the old man's innocuous appearance. Whichever Dorritt it was, he was engaged in nothing more sinister than emptying a bottle of milk into the sink.

Hodson holstered his gun. "What the hell's going on here?" he asked curiously.

"Thought you were sleeping," muttered the doorman.

"That's what you were supposed to think," said Hodson with a wink at Eliza. Let the old geezer think I set a trap for him, he thought, and hoped the girl wouldn't give away the game.

"Think I didn't catch on to why you kept coming up and offering to give me a break?" Even as he said it, Hodson realized that his words actually did match the facts. By damn, Dorritt *had* been back and forth all evening trying to get him away from the third floor! "But why this apartment and not the other one?" he asked.

"My job," the man answered sullenly. "Keep an eye on the place when tenants are gone."

"At three o'clock in the morning?" exclaimed Eliza.

Dorritt shrugged his thin shoulders inside his worn navy blue sweater.

"Okay," said Hodson. "That's it. Leave that bottle right there on the sink and let's go."

Mutely, Dorritt doused the lights. Hodson and Eliza followed him down the hall and at the front door, the policeman waited for him to lock up and then took the keys.

"Gotta have 'em," Dorritt protested.

"You can get 'em back from my sergeant or the lieutenant tomorrow," Hodson said heartlessly. "Now beat it!"

He looked at Eliza. "You, too, kid."

Dorritt punched the elevator button and Eliza had almost reached her aunt's door when she paused and said, "You don't smoke, do you, Mr. Dorritt?"

"What kind of a question's that?" growled Hodson.

Dorritt's natural inclination was to remain silent, but thinking it would annoy the policeman if he answered her, he shook his head and gave a negative grunt.

Thoughtfully, Eliza bolted and chained the door and trailed down the hallway.

"Eliza?"

Her heart sinking, Eliza opened the door to her aunt's room.

"Can't you sleep, dear?" murmured Aunt Elizabeth. "Why don't you prepare yourself a nice cup of cocoa?"

"I think I will," she answered gratefully. "Good night, Aunt Elizabeth."

"Sleep well, dear. And don't forget to turn off the stove."

CHAPTER 10

The telephone trilled next to Julie Redmond's bed and was echoed by an extension in the sunlit kitchen. Detective Tildon reluctantly pulled his attention from the dead woman's surprisingly complex bank records and carried his empty coffee cup down to the kitchen where he picked up the receiver on the fifth ring.

"Hello?" he answered cautiously, in case the caller was their still unidentified George.

"Couldn't resist it, could you, Tillie?" asked the lieutenant's voice.

"I finished those reports on the Harrison case before I came over," Tillie said defensively. "Left them on your desk. Anyhow," he added, "aren't you off duty?"

"Oh well," said Sigrid.

She had awakened earlier than usual, feeling at loose ends. Despite what she'd told Nauman the morning before, her apartment needed little cleaning. Roman Tramegra had taken over the vacuuming lately—"Must earn my keep," he said—so after she had spent an hour straightening and dusting and another hour at the laundromat, the day had stretched unappealingly before her. The *Times*'s Sunday crossword puzzles had been too easy this morning, Nauman was in Amsterdam, and she had seen the exhibit of illuminated manuscripts at the Morgan Library.

Nauman gone had nothing to do with her restlessness, she assured herself; but as long as she was in this mood, work was as good an activity as any, especially since she was technically off duty and could in good conscience ignore the paperwork piling up on her desk for the more agreeable aspects of her job.

"Give me the address of Redmond's cleaning woman and I'll stop by on my way over," she told Tillie.

"I'm glad you're coming," he said. "Something odd happened here last night."

Mrs. Ermaline Yow had shiny black eyes, wiry salt-and-pepper hair held back from her face by pink plastic combs, and a less than immaculate apartment. Still in her bathrobe, she led Sigrid inside, dumped the Sunday comics from the best chair, and carried an overflowing ashtray and several coffee cups from a cluttered end table over to an even more littered dining table.

" 'Scuse the mess," she said cheerfully, "but after I clean up for other people all week, I don't seem to have the heart to start in here. So Miz Redmond went and got herself killed? Who's keeping Timmy? Not his daddy, I bet."

"At present, he seems to be staying with the Cavatoris next door," said Sigrid.

"Now, they're nice people!" said Mrs. Yow. "Don't you just love Miz Cavatori? So friendly and nice-speaking. And just crazy about Timmy. Both of 'em are. They think the sun rises and sets in him. More'n you could really say for his own mother. Ah well," she sighed, "mustn't talk like that now."

On the contrary, Sigrid told her. Julie Redmond's character and personality were precisely what she wanted to hear about if Mrs. Yow wouldn't mind.

In the best of all possible worlds, Mrs. Yow might have made a good clinical psychologist. As it was, observing her fellow human beings' quirks and foibles was an enjoyable pastime. She readjusted one of the pink combs in her thick hair and settled back comfortably to answer Sigrid's questions.

Yes, she had been cleaning for Miz Redmond almost three years now, starting right after the baby came. Half a day, twice a week, Tuesday and Friday mornings. All day Thursday at Miss Fitzpatrick's and lordy, the difference between those two! The Redmond apartment was so stripped-down that she could vacuum and dust the whole place in forty-five minutes while it took that long just to clean the table tops in Miss Fitzpatrick's living room.

"Now she's a nice lady, too, but—"

"But what was Mrs. Redmond like herself?" asked Sigrid.

"Well, like I say, the work was easy enough, but she was particular. Knew right to the minute how much work a body could get through in a morning and she always had a list laid out of exactly what she wanted done and I had to cross it off when I'd done it.

"Sometimes, though, when Timmy was still a baby and fussy with his teeth, she'd tell me to take him out to the park or wheel him around the block till he went to sleep. She'd rather do the work herself than mess with him when he was cranky. That was when he was real small, though. These days, he's a quiet little thing. Guess he wouldn't dare not be the way she jumped on him when he got the least bit loud. Good thing Mr. and Miz Cavatori like having him come over so often. She thinks—*thought,* I guess I should say now—that Miz Cavatori was sorta bossy about telling her how to raise Timmy and she thought Mr. Cavatori was spoiling Timmy, but she'd never say it to their face, you know, because she wanted them to keep taking Timmy when she wanted to go out. Free babysitting anytime she asked. But if Timmy didn't do just like she said, she'd tell him he might get his way across the hall, but he'd better not try it out on her or she'd blister his bottom."

"Didn't Mr. Redmond object to her treatment of the boy?"

"*Him?*" Mrs. Yow snorted and tightened the belt of her

robe around her trim frame before disabusing the young lieutenant of such notions. "He never said boo to anybody. Besides, I don't reckon he even knows. They've been split up about a year now. Timmy was still a baby back then, sleeping most of the time when Mr. Redmond was home. I think Timmy's scared of him, too. When Miz Redmond wasn't telling Timmy *she* was going to spank him, she was telling him how his daddy'd give it to him good if he acted up around him."

Sigrid remembered the way Timmy had shied away from Tillie and that Mrs. Cavatori had said he was afraid of all men except her husband. Was that because of Karl Redmond? And how did Redmond feel to see his own son shrink away from him with such terror? Bryna Leighton had hinted at the strained relationship. Was Redmond bitter or resigned about it, and did he blame himself or his ex-wife? Something else to look into.

"Did Mrs. Redmond know someone named George?" she asked.

"George?" Mrs. Yow scratched the side of her head thoughtfully with one of the pink combs. "There was a George Somebody or other that she used to work for up until Timmy was born. Washington? No, that's not right. Jefferson? The reason I know is that he called her up a lot around the time she was getting her divorce.

"I thought maybe she might be going to marry him, but then she just seemed to drop him flat, 'cause one Tuesday morning, she was out and he must have called a dozen times. When she came back and I gave her his messages, she just shrugged her shoulders and made a face like she didn't care if she ever talked to him again or not. And before that she'd been sweet as sugar when he called. What *was* that man's name? Madison?"

She jabbed the comb back into her hair, annoyed by her inability to fit a last name. "Oh well, just go to where she used to work. They'll tell you."

"Can you suggest anyone who might have wanted Mrs. Redmond dead?" asked Sigrid.

Mrs. Yow shook her head. "I don't think she had any good enough friends for that."

She paused and observed shrewdly, "Sounds funny when you say it like that, doesn't it? But she sure wasn't one to hang on the telephone. Least, not when I was there. I think she went shopping by herself and nobody ever dropped in for a cup of coffee neither, unless you count her brother, and she didn't like it if he came while I was there."

"Were they close?"

"Well, it seemed like they were when he started coming around last spring. First couple of weeks, he was there almost every morning I was. Then she must have said something, 'cause he started waiting till just as I was leaving. A couple of times though, she made me take Timmy to the park 'cause she said they had some business to discuss. About the divorce, I reckon.

"That was just before poor old Mr. Redmond was killed and the business went bust. I could hear the two of 'em almost every Thursday through Miss Fitzpatrick's kitchen wall. Thick as thieves they were. But then after her and Mr. Redmond got divorced, he didn't seem to come around as much, and when he did, I don't know. It was like—" Mrs. Yow searched for a graphic analogy.

"You know how it feels in the summer before we get one of those bad thunder and lightning storms? When it's so heavy-feeling you need to take a deep breath every couple of minutes? Well, that's the way it felt to be in the same room with Miz Redmond and that brother of hers all last summer."

For a long moment, she thought about what she'd just put into words, then she looked at Sigrid in puzzled surprise. "You know something? It sounds terrible to say this about a brother and sister; but yeah, he just might have wanted her dead. I don't know—somehow I used to have the feeling that she had something that belonged to him and wouldn't give it back.

"What if he just killed her and took it?"

CHAPTER 11

By ten-thirty, the bright May morning had gone from mild springtime to a warm reminder that summer's heat lurked just around the next turn of a calendar page.

Sigrid parked half a block down from the Rensselaer Building and left her gray suit jacket slung across the front seat. As she emerged from the car in a long-sleeved white shirt and a dark blue vest over loose gray slacks, it occurred to her that perhaps she should have spent the day packing away winter clothes and airing out her summer wardrobe, which was at least lighter in weight and texture if not in colors.

Meeting the Cavatoris and Timmy Redmond on the sidewalk only underlined the point.

Timmy wore short white pants and a little red blazer and he clung to Vico Cavatori, who wore a well-cut light brown suit. But it was Mrs. Cavatori who made Sigrid self-consciously aware of how out of season her wool clothes were.

If Luisa Cavatori lived to be a hundred, she would still be making the most of her physical attractions. She'd never been thin, not even in her girlhood, but plumpness hadn't led her into the sort of timid styling and unobtrusive colors other generously endowed women so often adopt. All her life she had been complacent about her vigorous beauty and had dressed with a style and flair that still turned male heads of all ages.

Looking like a firm and juicy apple today, Mrs. Cavatori wore a green linen coatdress piped in crisp white. Shoes and purse matched perfectly. A twisted circlet of white chiffon did hat duty on her sleek dark hair and her gloved hands carried a prayer book and rosary.

She did not immediately place the young woman who had paused before them. Automatically, her shrewd brown eyes cataloged the shapeless clothes—good enough quality, but so drab. Such a waste, too, because *Dio mio,* look at those bones! Like one of those girls who had modeled their spring line of tennis dresses back in January. Loosen that hair, add some liner to those eyes...

The penny dropped with those gray eyes, and Luisa Cavatori recognized the lieutenant who had come to ask them about Julie yesterday. And here she'd been taking the girl and her clothes apart in her mind! And that one, she knew it, no? A little redder in those thin cheeks?

Regretting her unintentional rudeness, Luisa Cavatori gave the younger woman a kindly smile. After all, how should a policewoman know about clothes?

Sigrid's flush deepened as she perceived the charity in Mrs. Cavatori's smile and she tried to cover her awkwardness by addressing the child.

"Hello, Timmy. Going to church this morning?"

He held Mr. Cavatori's hand tighter, but nodded shyly. "An' the zoo," he whispered.

Vico Cavatori cupped the boy's head with a gentle hand and smiled at Sigrid. "But first we go to church. To light candles for Timmy's new little sister."

"Born last night," explained Mrs. Cavatori with a graceful shrug and an expressive roll of her eyes which conveyed blame for the parents while acknowledging the baby's innocence, all in one humorous gesture.

Sigrid could not restrain an answering smile, and Luisa

Cavatori tilted her head in the sunlight and gave a gurgle of rich laughter as she impulsively clasped the younger woman's hand.

"Ah, Lieutenant Harald! Such a world as we live in today, no?" Then, more seriously, she said, "Do you come again to ask us questions? I will go back up with you if you wish it."

She consulted her frail husband. "You will be all right, *caro?*"

Over Mr. Cavatori's assurances that he and Timmy could manage alone nicely, Sigrid explained that she was only joining Detective Tildon for an examination of Mrs. Redmond's papers this morning, not conducting more interviews.

"At least not at the moment," she told them. "I don't guarantee that I won't need your help again later."

Vico Cavatori was courtly as he insisted that they were at the lieutenant's service whenever she wished. He had been surprised by the charm of Sigrid's spontaneous smile. Ah, but when, he reflected, did Luisa's warmth *not* melt through all resistance?

His eyes met hers above Timmy's head and he was seized by a moment of absolute clarity. A crystal awareness of the long years behind them, an acceptance of death's nearness; but more than either, a reaffirmation that for such a woman he would do it all again. Everything. He would change nothing—none of their struggles during the war, none of their pain afterward—nothing so long as they were together.

"*Caro?*" she murmured.

"*Niente,*" he smiled.

To tell her these things now would only alarm her—make her worry that another heart attack was imminent.

Timmy held a hand of each and now he tugged at them and laughed up at their indulgent faces.

"I-me light a candle?"

"*Ma sicuro,*" said Vico. "We will *all* light candles for our blessings. *Andiamo!*"

• • •

There was no sign of either Dorritt twin when Sigrid passed through the lobby. Up on the third floor, Hodson's relief stood up to intercept her, then saluted smartly as she flipped open her ID without breaking stride. The front door to apartment 3-D was slightly ajar, and she entered unheard by the two people in Julie Redmond's living room.

His back to the door, Detective Tildon was at the white desk, bringing order to bills, canceled checks, and tax statements, while a girl of fragile appearance sat cross-legged on the carpet at his feet.

It was a very expensive carpet. A rich border of apricot, burnt orange, and yellow flowers edged the pale cream ground. The girl might be dressed in jeans, but she looked as if she were used to taking silk carpets for granted. Of course, the jeans did sport a designer label and were topped by a hand-embroidered batiste shirt. Her light brown hair was held back from a small-boned face by two long thin braids and a cloisonné barrette. A couple of gold chains, one partially strung with graduated gold beads, glinted at the neckline of her shirt.

Sigrid was just in time to hear Eliza Fitzpatrick ask, "How did you feel the first time a woman gave you a direct order?"

Tillie shrugged. "Angry, I suppose. And rebellious probably."

"How did you handle it?" the girl pressed.

"I did as I was told," said Tillie. "I picked up my toys, put them in my toybox, and went to bed."

"That's *not* what I meant! And you *know*—Oh! Lieutenant Harald," she said, scrambling to her feet in obvious delight. "Neat! I was hoping you'd come before Aunt Elizabeth got back from church."

Tillie's pink cheeks went even pinker as he realized that the lieutenant must have overheard his last remark. He rather thought she had a sense of humor, but so far he hadn't the confidence to take it for granted. Her gaze was mildly inquiring and he answered cautiously, "Miss Fitzpatrick came to offer her assistance."

His instinct was confirmed by just the slightest glint of amusement in the young woman's slate gray eyes. She became even more formal. Such a reaction, Tillie was learning, meant that she was prepared to enjoy the humor in a situation.

"You were a close friend of Mrs. Redmond's?" she asked. "Knew her well?"

At fifteen, Eliza was too much like her great-aunt to have mastered much duplicity. She laughed outright at the idea of being Julie Redmond's confidante.

"See? You *do* need my help. You can't have too clear a picture of her if you seriously believe Julie had any close female friends. Let alone somebody still in high school like me. I'm as intelligent as anybody twice my age," she said. It was a statement of fact, not a boast. "But Julie wasn't exactly the sort of person you'd ever discuss ideas with. I mean, she was only interested in *things.*

"Most of the time the Cavatoris kept Timmy when she was going out, but I sat with him once in a while when they had to be away at the same time, and all I ever heard Julie talk about were things she wanted to buy—clothes, makeup, or furniture, stuff like that—or men. Especially men."

Eliza's eyes dropped, then her chin came up determinedly. "I saw what you were thinking about my father yesterday."

"Did you?" Sigrid answered neutrally.

"You thought he wasn't telling the truth about not knowing Julie," she accused.

Sigrid said nothing.

"You've got the wrong impression of him," Eliza said. "Dad may be uptight, but he's not repressed."

A small strangled sound escaped from Tillie, and Sigrid turned a cold eye upon him. "Is there any more of that coffee?"she asked pointedly.

Lips twitching, Tillie grabbed his cup and escaped to the kitchen.

"In a way, I guess it *is* funny," Eliza said. "As far as Dad's concerned, women are either ladies or tramps. There's no middle ground. And I think Julie used sex to get what she wanted. Any time a man got within fifty feet, her body just put itself on automatic. She couldn't help it."

Eliza paused, then added thoughtfully, "I guess it was like one of those positive-feedback experiments we did in biology class last fall: If something works, you keep trying it.

"Anyhow, I think she gave Dad the come-on once when they happened to ride down in the elevator together. Knowing Dad, his reaction probably insulted her and instead of ignoring him after that, whenever they met, she seemed to go out of her way to needle him."

"How?"

"Silly things. She'd ask him if there was a run at the back of her stockings so he'd have to look at her legs; or she'd pretend to have a pebble in her shoe and have to hang onto his arm to keep her balance while she took her shoe off. Sometimes she'd slip her wrist under his nose and ask him if he thought the perfume was sexier than what she'd been wearing last time. You'd have to know Dad to know how much this sort of thing bugged him.

"Oh, and once she made one of the doormen ride up in the elevator with them like she was afraid to go up alone with Dad. He was furious and told Mom that the doorman was muttering under his breath about sex maniacs. Mom said if he'd pinch Julie's bottom one time, she'd probably leave him alone; but for Dad, that was a case of the cure being worse than the disease."

"So your father won't be Mrs. Redmond's chief mourner?"

"But that doesn't mean he would hurt her," Eliza protested.

Insulated by the egocentrism of youth, Eliza Fitzpatrick had been relatively unmoved by Julie Redmond's murder. There had been no meeting of minds in the two or three times she'd sat for the woman, no touching of sympathetic chords. Eliza was scornful of women who used their bodies instead of their minds and she'd lumped Julie into that category as casually and as completely as had her father.

Gilbert Fitzpatrick's exasperation with Julie's harassment had seemed funny to her. Eliza knew that her father was stuffy and humorless; on the whole, though, she loved and admired him and she planned to follow his footsteps into law school with the significant exception of specializing in criminal law rather than civil or corporate.

Julie's death had seemed like a terrific opportunity to gather firsthand information about a murder investigation. That the officer in charge happened to be a competent, no-nonsense woman only added to its interest. Last night had been half scary but exciting; yet watching the lieutenant coolly analyze what she'd just said about her father brought Eliza to the abrupt realization that this was not some abstract game of hypothetical probabilities. Julie had been killed yesterday morning, and this woman's job was to bring somebody—anybody?—to trial for it.

"Anyhow," she said quickly, "Dad has a standing squash game with a friend every Saturday morning."

His grin under control, Detective Tildon returned with three cups of coffee and a more professional air. He tactfully elicited the name of Gilbert Fitzpatrick's squash partner without alarming the girl.

"Miss Fitzpatrick seems to have had a busy night, too," said Tillie, handing Sigrid a written précis of Hodson's carefully edited version of last night's events. Hodson's relief had passed it along to Tillie this morning along with Dorritt's key ring.

Sigrid sipped her coffee and skimmed through the account. She glanced at Eliza Fitzpatrick, who looked somewhat embarrassed by Tillie's words.

"I couldn't sleep," Eliza explained, "so I got up to make some hot chocolate to relax me and I just thought I'd see if Officer Hodson wanted some, too—and *please* don't say anything about it to Aunt Elizabeth or in front of my father or mother!"

They assured the girl of their discretion and, after hearing her account of the doorman's early morning activity, sat back, puzzled.

"Hodson says one of the Dorritts offered to relieve him several times during the evening," mused Tillie. "Once to go out for a sandwich, again to use the john in the basement, and finally just to go up to the roof and stretch his legs. Very considerate."

"Certainly doesn't sound like the Dorritts we've come

to know and love," Sigrid agreed. "But why 3-A? Did Hodson check out the whole apartment?"

Tillie shrugged, and Eliza, who'd listened enthralled, said, "No, he didn't. Just made Mr. Dorritt leave everything as it was and come away. And something else, Lieutenant—the Bitzers have been away for a couple of weeks, but I smelled cigarette smoke in the service hall, and Mr. Dorritt says he doesn't smoke."

"That was very observant of you," said Sigrid, pleased. Her gray eyes flicked over to Tillie, then back again to the girl. "Would you mind being present while we question the Dorritt brothers?"

"I'd *love*—I mean," said Eliza, struggling for dignity, "I'll be glad to help any way I can."

Tillie's lips were twitching again as he departed in search of the Bobbsey twins.

CHAPTER 12

The morning after too much cocaine is not like the morning after too much alcohol. One's head does not throb with the slightest movement, one can think of last night's dinner without lurching for the bathroom, and one does not necessarily resort to the hair of the dog in order to stabilize the shakes. Nevertheless, the lambent spring sunlight which streamed through faded curtains did nothing to warm Mickey Novak's spirits.

To the uninitiated, his drippy nose, streaming red eyes, and stuffy head might seem like symptoms of hay fever or a common spring cold, but Novak was bleakly aware of the difference. Ordinarily he was not a heavy user, but last night he'd wanted to blot out everything. Today, he had awakened jittery and anxious in a strange room and it had taken him several minutes to get his bearings.

This particular room might not be familiar, but its tired wallpaper, bare floors, and cheap, minimal furnishings made it the counterpart of a thousand others throughout the city. It could have been the same boardinghouse he'd so hastily moved out of yesterday afternoon.

The room was not particularly dirty; it was, in fact, cleaner than many he'd lived in. All the same, there was a grayness here that would never come bright again and a musty, dusty smell of Lysol and homelessness.

He and Julie had begun in rooms like this. That foster home where the social workers had stuck the two Novak kids had been an apartment of dingy gray rooms.

But Julie had gotten out. And once in a while, when she was between guys and he was between reform schools or prison, she'd let him move in for a few weeks.

With almost physical longing, he thought of Julie's apartment—nothing faded or secondhand. Everything new and clean. Every object chosen to set off Julie's soft black hair and her clear skin: sheer white curtains, bright cushions on that orangy-pink couch, cut-glass bowls of yellow flowers. All gone now . . . gone for good.

At twenty-four, Mickey Novak had wasted little time on sentimentality or introspection, but as he paced the linoleum he was filled with a wrenching sense of loss.

Julie could be a real bitch, he thought—a cold-hearted, lying, double-dealing bitch—but he'd never wanted her dead. Not really. Okay, maybe he'd belted her once or twice. God knows she'd deserved it. She played rough herself and if anybody else had pulled that, he'd have killed them long ago. After what Julie'd been through as a kid, though, maybe she needed all the softness and smooth things money could buy. Besides, she'd only done to him what he might have done to her if he'd thought of it first.

He tried to calm himself, knowing that this nervous agitation came as much from snorting coke last night as from what happened yesterday. He hadn't been this shook-up yesterday. He'd stayed calm, found the key, and got away clean.

Not too clean, he remembered irritably, and looked at his black boots. Flecks of green paint still clung to the instep despite the swabbing he'd given them with lighter fluid last night. He'd have to throw them away. They'd tie him to Julie's apartment house if the police caught up with him.

Looking for another pair, he unsnapped the catches of a large brown leather suitcase; $189.95 it'd cost. Genuine pigskin, and he hadn't stolen it, either. He'd paid cash over

the counter for it in a regular store with part of the thirty
thousand Julie'd given him. Inside was everything he
owned at the moment; the things he'd brought with him
when he decided he'd better clear out of the last place before
the cops got onto him from his parole officer—a few
changes of clothes, some toilet articles, a radio/cassette
player with a dozen or so tapes, some other odds and ends,
and a bundle of birthday cards.

Funny those cards. No matter where he was, Julie'd
always mailed him one. Or got him one and hung onto it
till she knew where he was.

He fumbled for a handkerchief, blew his nose, and
damned the coke. It was the coke that made his eyes stream
like this. He'd never cried over anybody or anything—no,
not even that first time they'd hauled him off to juvenile
hall and that Spanish kid took his jacket and threatened to
kick his teeth out if he told. Not even then. But low moans
escaped through his clenched teeth now as he turned the
cards over and over in agitated hands.

They were all gag cards, but he'd come to count on them
through the years. They'd never kissed or hugged. The
only time she'd ever touched him was to slap his face a
couple of times.

But she sent the cards.

And once—the year he was nineteen—he'd been sleeping
on her couch all week and when he came in that night, she
had a cake from the bakery down the street and there were
nineteen blue candles on it and she'd even got him a present,
a silver chain with a little silver horseshoe that he'd worn
until some girl lifted it. It was the first glimpse he'd ever
had of what regular families must be like, but they fought
the next day and she threw him out and the week after
that he was picked up and took a six-month fall for second-
degree burglary.

But how could she be dead? He hadn't wanted that. She
was his sister. His only relative. They hadn't had the same
old man and their mother had abandoned them before he
could remember her, but Julie'd always been there, somewhere where he could call her up even if she was calling
him a bum and a jailbird ten minutes later.

Those few weeks before her marriage to Redmond went

bust had been some of the happiest he'd ever had. They'd been close then, like a real brother and sister. Planning together what it'd be like after Redmond was out of the way.

He'd thought she'd be giving Redmond that whiny brat, but she'd hung onto him.

"What do you want the kid for?" he'd asked her.

"He's why the judge gave me the apartment," she'd laughed.

"And don't forget all that lovely child-support money coming in every month."

"But you don't need it," he'd argued. "You've got more money now than you'll ever spend." And that was before he'd known she was going to keep it all. He should have known from the way her eyes had narrowed so coldly.

"There's never too much money, Mickey. I'm never going back to furnished rooms again as long as I live."

And then she'd cheated him out of his part and laughed in his face. Now it would all be his again; but oh damn! Julie was dead and all the money in the world couldn't buy someone to send him birthday cards.

"Come on, George! You're not even trying!"

George Franklin made an amiable *mea culpa* gesture and loped after the missed tennis ball.

It was the third time in a row that he'd failed to get his racket on it, much less send it back across the net to her. Exasperated, Sue Montrose watched him scoop up a couple of their balls that had rolled to the fence. He moved gracefully and his body certainly looked athletic enough in white knit shirt and white tennis shorts. He had dark curly hair, lightly muscled arms and legs, and sported a deep tan. How could someone so handsome look like a pro and yet play like a—a *poodle*?

She silently apologized to all the slandered poodles of the world. At least they'll fetch the ball back when you throw it, she thought, which is more than you can say for George.

"Okay, Billie Jean, here it comes!" he warned, and

served a fairly crisp smash to her right. In this case, since
Sue was left-handed, the serve was to her backhand.

Actually, thought George, she did look a little like a
young Billie Jean King. She was small and sturdily built
and reddish-brown hair covered her head in short curls.
Not at all like the leggy beauties with flowing hair he
usually chose.

He'd never seen Billie Jean King up close, so he didn't
know if she was freckled all over like Susie; but they both
tucked their tongues in the corner of their mouths when
competing and both had similar smiles.

Except that Sue hadn't done much smiling today. Hell,
she knew he wasn't a jock. Why was she getting so uptight
about the way he was playing today?

He stepped into his swing, kept his racket level for a
change, and sent the ball deep into her right court. By
focusing strictly on tennis, he could keep her scampering
around the court happily enough. She really didn't mind
his erratic returns—even if they were out of bounds—as
long as they fell somewhere within her reach.

Usually there was a look of serious and utter absorption
on her face as she concentrated on form and placement; it
was that look that had first attracted him in the early days
of their relationship. He'd not been used to women block-
ing him out so totally. Getting past that straight-lipped
reserve had been a challenge.

Since grade school and puberty, he'd noticed that girls
were electrically aware of him. Julie, too. Even when she
was using him, she couldn't blank out the natural attraction
between them.

God! What a body she had. Even after a kid and four
years of marriage. It was a body still worth taking chances
for, but did she really think he was stupid enough to let
himself get caught by a tap he'd installed himself?

"*George!*"

Startled, he flailed wildly at the white ball that was zing-
ing straight for his head and managed to duck before he
was brained.

"Sorry, doll," he called. "I lost it in the sun."

CHAPTER 13

Muttering antiphonal complaints, the Dorritt twins had resentfully accepted Lieutenant Harald's invitation to tour the Bitzer apartment, and they might have denied being caught there if Eliza Fitzpatrick hadn't brightly showed Sigrid the empty bottle of milk on the kitchen sink. The Dorritts looked lugubriously at the bottle, at each other, and back to Sigrid again.

"Is emptying a tenant's milk part of your janitorial duties?" she asked pleasantly.

Again each head had waggled and dipped silently.

There was no sign of intrusion in any other part of the living quarters of the large, luxuriously furnished apartment. The Bitzers seemed to be archaeology buffs, for there were glass cases of neolithic pottery and projectile points; and bits of marble statuary from all over the world were displayed in every room, most of them too fragmentary and flawed to be true museum pieces.

As Eliza had noticed earlier in the small hours of the morning, there was definitely a strong smell of stale cigarette smoke in the back hall. A tall bar stool and an overturned ashtray at the end of the hall next to the service door had told their own story.

The Dorritt twins now sat side by side on the apricot velvet couch in apartment 3-D, stubbornly uncooperative.

Sigrid was beginning to sort them out. Manny, the one she'd talked to yesterday, had a small strip of adhesive tape on the loose folds of wrinkled skin under his chin and it seemed to be his turn to wear the official doorman's jacket this morning.

Except for a dark navy version of his brother's maroon cardigan and the fact that his deep-set pale blue eyes were slightly more bloodshot, Sammy Dorritt was a mirror image. Those red-rimmed eyes indicated loss of sleep and made him a good choice for Hodson's peripatetic visitor.

Not for one minute had there been the slightest doubt in either Sigrid or Tillie's mind that Hodson had been sound asleep when whichever Dorritt it was had come up the last time. If not for Eliza Fitzpatrick, he'd have come and gone with them none the wiser. As a reward, Eliza received unofficial permission to stay. It might be a little unorthodox and certainly it hadn't been spelled out in so many words, but Eliza had been given to understand that as long as she stayed out from underfoot, neither Detective Tildon nor Lieutenant Harald would be inclined to chase her away.

With a little luck, Eliza thought happily, Aunt Elizabeth might stop off for a cup of tea with some of her church friends before coming home. In the meantime, she curled up in one of the gold-and-white wingback chairs across the room and waited for Lieutenant Harald to learn who the Bitzers' first intruder had been.

Patiently, Sigrid pointed out that there was no sign that the door to 3-A had been forced. To whom, she asked again, had they given a passkey?

"Bitzers have extra keys," said Sammy.

"Sublet the place last year," added Manny.

It would help if their heads moved in unison, Tillie decided. You could follow them easier. Instead, the iron gray heads on each long neck bobbed and ducked independently. When the brothers silently communed with each other, they seemed to be nodding constant agreement in uneven syncopation.

Sigrid ignored the dipping heads and said, "You've heard me send for a technical unit. It will only take a few hours to run your friend's fingerprints through the computer; so you might as well save us all a little time and tell us his name now."

"He could be an important witness," Tillie coaxed. "Maybe even tell us who killed Mrs. Redmond."

The Dorritts were mute.

"If you cooperate, we may not have to inform the Bitzers how you gave somebody free run of their apartment. On the other hand," he warned, "obstruction of justice is a serious charge. Especially since there's no need of it. Like the lieutenant said—as soon as we run a fingerprint check, we'll know anyhow."

Manny Dorritt looked indifferent to the threat, which argued against any previous criminal activity on the part of whoever had sat on that stool long enough to fill an ashtray with cigarette butts; but there seemed to be a slight uneasiness on Sammy's gaunt face.

"Bonded last year," he reminded his twin. "Security clearance."

"Fingerprints?" asked Manny.

Sammy Dorritt's head dipped and salaamed in confirmation.

Manny Dorritt hunched his thin shoulders and bit the bullet. "She didn't see nothing."

Tillie was surprised. "*She?*"

"Her full name and address, please," Sigrid said calmly, not wishing to scare them back into silence.

Grudgingly, the Dorritts parted with an Upper West Side address and a name: Sue Montrose.

"Niece," they said, and that was as far as they could or would go in explaining why they'd given her a key. If they knew why Sue Montrose had wanted to spend her Saturday morning watching the third-floor vestibule, they weren't admitting it.

In the end, Sigrid let them go; and while Tillie went back to straightening Julie Redmond's ransacked papers, she went down to the kitchen to dial the telephone number Manny Dorritt had provided.

"Miss Montrose, please," she said when a feminine voice answered on the first ring.

"Sorry, she and George are playing tennis. This is her roommate. Want to leave a message?"

"It's rather important that I talk to her," said Sigrid. "When do you expect her back?"

"Who knows? They only left about ten minutes ago. I think the court was booked for noon. Hang on a minute, okay?"

She was back shortly with the location of the Central Park tennis court where her roommate might be found.

Thoughtfully, Sigrid returned to the living room. Tillie was as intrigued as she to learn that Sue Montrose's tennis partner was named George.

"Want me to come with you?" Tillie asked, his hands full of MasterCard statements.

"No, one of us ought to be here when the lab men arrive next door," she decided. "Besides, you don't really want to leave that desk, do you?"

Things were starting to get interesting, Tillie admitted. "I should have everything sorted in another half hour and then I can really get into putting the pieces together. She seems to have had an awful lot of money."

"No job and she was getting what in child support?" mused Sigrid. "Five hundred a month?"

Across the room, Eliza Fitzpatrick stirred in her chair. "Julie certainly didn't live on just that! Why just last week she had on a new suit that was advertised at Bloomingdale's for four hundred and sixty dollars."

"*Four hundred and sixty dollars!*" Sigrid almost never read fashion ads. To augment her Carolina clothes, she followed Anne through designer lofts or to specialty thrift shops where society's fashionable shed the distinctive clothes they couldn't be seen in more than once or twice. The most expensive item in Sigrid's closet was a cashmere coat that she'd paid three hundred dollars for and had felt terribly extravagant about ever since.

Tillie grinned at her horrified expression and pulled

another charge statement from the heap in front of him.

"Can I help?" Eliza asked shyly. "I don't have anything to do until Aunt Elizabeth gets home."

Tillie glanced at Sigrid, who nodded that it was all right with her. "You do know what privileged information is though, don't you?" she asked the girl.

"It means I don't tell anybody about anything you've let me see or hear this morning." She took the pile of bills Tillie handed her and began arranging them by date and category.

"You've forgotten my father's a lawyer," she reminded Sigrid.

"And you're a credit to his calling?" Sigrid asked dryly as she gathered up her things to go.

Eliza caught the tone and gave her a delighted grin. "I certainly do try to be," she said with mock demureness.

About twenty minutes later, she handed Tillie a slip of paper. "You said to mention anything odd, so what about this?"

It was a jeweler's bill dated just over a year ago and acknowledged payment for a key-shaped charm made to order from fourteen-karat gold.

"What's odd about it?" asked Tillie.

"Well, look how expensive it is to get something specially made like that," said Eliza. "Why didn't she just get Karl to make it? He and his father still owned their own jewelry store then."

"Maybe it was a gift, a surprise for him," said Tillie, who was very happily married.

Eliza shook her head. "No, this was hers. She wore it all the time—a gold chain with a little heart-shaped lock and a key. This key. And something else: They didn't really match. The key had the same sort of filigree on top, but the size was wrong. It was too big for the heart. Not that it really mattered. Most of the time you never saw it because the chain was long and hung down inside her clothes. But why would she spend this much money for something that was off?"

"She wore it all the time?" asked Tillie. He was beginning to remember something.

"I think so," said Eliza. "She told me it was her good-luck necklace."

Tillie knew that a jewelry box with several expensive pieces remained in the bedroom, so they had not thought that robbery played a part in the Redmond death. Yet they had found no gold chain with a heart and key in that box and nothing around the dead woman's neck except that abrasion Cohen had showed them.

"You're right," he told Eliza, carefully setting the bill aside. "Maybe this *is* odd."

CHAPTER 14

Notwithstanding dirty buses, unsafe subways, and steadily rising fares, New York is officially committed to public transportation. Private automobiles are allowed, of course, but not encouraged. Doubters may examine the state of New York's streets or take a spin on its expressways.

During the day, street parking is virtually banned from the East River to the Hudson between Twenty-third and Seventy-second streets; elsewhere, alternate sides of the street offer occasional havens if one can keep up with which days are safe and which are *verboten*.

Most of the rules are relaxed on the weekends, and the city becomes more tolerant. With police identification on her car tags, Sigrid did not have to worry about being towed, but she preferred to park legally whenever that was possible. Accordingly, she counted herself lucky when a Volkswagen van pulled away from the curb on Central Park West not too far from the West Ninety-sixth Street entrance to the park.

The hot noon sun had brought out crowds of Sunday strollers, and joggers in shorts and sweatbands, cyclists with babies strapped into baskets fore and aft, skateboarders, and roller-skaters zipped by her as she turned into the park. Her long strides overtook a contingent of beer-bellied softball players resplendent in gold and crimson uniforms.

Sigrid did not run, cycle, or play team games; but she saw a croquet game in progress upon a grassy flat and was instantly transported back to the wet summer day when she and her cousins had waited out the rain by rummaging in Grandmother Lattimore's vast attic. They had found a brass-bound croquet set that their grandparents had brought home from their wedding trip to London.

For the rest of that visit and for several summers thereafter through her teens, they had turned Grandmother Lattimore's west lawn into a free-form croquet court. It was discovered that the skinny Yankee cousin, somewhat bookish and almost painfully shy, had a killer instinct when it came to croquet, and the cousins fought to be her partner. An elaborate handicap system had to be worked out so that everyone stood a chance of winning their flat-out, no-holds-barred version of the game.

As Sigrid moved on, her gray eyes, usually so clear and purposeful, were almost dreamy as she remembered the brambled rosebushes that edged Grandmother Lattimore's west lawn, the many-stemmed crepe myrtle tree in the middle of the course, and an iron deer that required a tricky bank shot off a set of stone steps to get around it.

The tennis courts were full and, on benches behind the chain-link fence, other players waited their turns. There was something joyous and carefree about the thwack of rackets upon balls and balls upon the courts.

Sigrid found the court attendant, who consulted his list and told her that Sue Montrose was supposed to be playing on the end court. He checked his watch and added, "Her time's up in eight minutes."

Pleased to have a chance to study Montrose and her companion unobserved, Sigrid threaded her way through the onlookers to the far court. She'd subconsciously expected the Dorritt twins' niece to be middle-aged, tall, and skinny. Instead, she found a very attractive girl in her early twenties, with a nicely rounded body that barely topped five-three.

Score one more point for the mysteries of genetics,

thought Sigrid, and leaned against an iron stanchion to watch the finish of their game.

The Montrose girl might be small, but she packed a wallop with her racket. Left-handed though, Sigrid saw, and Cohen said that Julie Redmond's death blow had probably been dealt by someone right-handed. Besides, Redmond had been rather tall. Even seated she probably would have been a difficult target for Montrose.

On the other hand, George—the George of Julie Redmond's tape?—was a hair over six feet, right-handed, and was, Sigrid noted clinically, one of the most physically stunning men she'd ever seen. Knew it, too, she thought, sensing a self-consciousness about the man's movements when he missed a ball and had to come down to the fence to retrieve it. His eyes raked her automatically as he passed nearby. Sigrid was used to not stopping a man's eye and this time it didn't bother her because she had the impression that this man's eyes never stopped roving. Even now he was grandstanding ever so slightly for a gorgeous redhead posed just behind the fence.

Was that what explained the withdrawn expression on Sue Montrose's freckled face? She seemed cool and unruffled and she was punishing the man subtly, making him look faintly inept as she peppered the court with well-laced shots that looked easy but were just out of his reach. He was sweating and panting and starting to sulk. When the court attendant called time on them, he slung his towel around his neck and stomped off to the water fountain without looking back.

Calmly, the girl gathered up their balls, put them back in a tin, slipped on a white cardigan, and picked up the man's sweater and racket cover. Sigrid met her at the gate.

"Miss Montrose?"

"Yes?"

"I'm Lieutenant Herald," she said, flipping open her ID case. "I'm investigating Julie Redmond's death and would like to ask you a few questions about yesterday morning."

The girl's brown eyes widened and she risked a quick glance at the man who was just straightening from the water fountain. Hastily, she separated his belongings from hers, placed them on a nearby bench and called to him, "I have to leave now, George; I'll phone you tonight."

She turned back to Sigrid and tried to keep her voice matter of fact. "Shall we go, Lieutenant?"

"Oh, there's no hurry," Sigrid said vaguely. She realized that Sue Montrose would prefer to keep the man out of it. He, on the other hand, had stopped dawdling and was returning faster than he'd originally intended.

George Franklin was too self-centered to be the most perceptive of lovers, but he was sufficiently attuned to Sue's moods to know she was now uptight about something more than his casual flirtation with that redhead. He saw that she had gone white beneath her freckles and seemed almost afraid of the tall, angular woman who had joined her.

"Something wrong, Susie?" he asked, moving protectively closer.

Resigned, Sue said, "Julie Redmond was killed yesterday and this police officer wants to ask me some questions."

"Killed? You mean *murdered?* Julie?"

Sigrid said, "I believe you knew Mrs. Redmond also, Mr.—?"

"Franklin," he said automatically. "George Franklin."

Which explained Mrs. Yow's groping through a roster of the Founding Fathers, thought Sigrid.

"What do you want with Sue?" Franklin asked.

Sigrid decided to force the situation. "Mrs. Redmond was killed in her apartment and we think Miss Montrose may have been there yesterday," she said deliberately.

Sigrid watched the stunned look on his face. Because Julie Redmond had been killed or because Sue Montrose had been there?

George grasped the girl's arm. "Why didn't you tell me?"

She stared back at him with level brown eyes. "I didn't know you still kept in touch with her." She handed him his sweater and he put it on mechanically.

"Well, I didn't. Not really." His own eyes wavered uneasily, then he said firmly, "I haven't seen Julie since last fall."

"She once worked for you, Mr. Franklin?" Sigrid asked.

"My secretary. She quit when she got married four years ago."

"But you knew her socially, too?"

Sue Montrose had gone even whiter and George Franklin was now visibly uncomfortable. "Not since she was married," he insisted. "She kept in touch. Phone calls once in a while, and drinks one time after work a few months back, but that's all!"

"And you didn't visit her yesterday morning?"

"Of course not. I was"—there was a split-second hesitation—"I was at my dentist's."

He answered her questions, but the words were directed at his companion, who seemed intent now on watching the players who had replaced them on the court.

Sigrid looked from one to the other and said briskly, "Then I won't detain you any longer, Mr. Franklin."

"Now wait a minute! I'm not going to leave Sue alone here for you to bully and—"

"It's okay, George," Sue said.

"No, it's not. Why does she think you were there? You don't even like Julie."

"You're forgetting that my uncles work in her building," she said. "I was the one who told her about the apartment in the first place, remember?"

"Yes, but—"

"Look, George, why don't you go back to my place? Ask Jenny to give you a drink. This shouldn't take long. Please?"

He went reluctantly, his handsome face as sulky as a child's when sent to play while grown-ups talk. Sigrid was happy to take advantage of the girl's readiness to cooperate and pointed to a vacant bench on a rise above the crowded tennis courts.

"I don't know if I can be much help," said Sue Montrose as they sat down. "It's true that I visited my uncles yesterday morning, but I didn't know Julie all that well and—" Her voice died away as she met Sigrid's cool gray eyes, and her freckled face turned bright pink.

"We know that you were watching from the Bitzer apartment for several hours," Sigrid said kindly.

"How?" she whispered.

"Your uncles were caught trying to clear away your traces."

Sue Montrose sighed. "They're grumpy old dears. They must have hated getting caught. I guess I wasn't thinking too clearly. Just grabbed my bag and ran."

"Why were you there in the first place?"

She took a deep breath and gave a shaky little laugh. "Jealousy pure and simple, Lieutenant. You heard George. She was his secretary before me and I thought he was seeing her again."

"You're Mr. Franklin's secretary, too?" Surprise made Sigrid tactless.

The girl colored again. "George is a creature of habit," she said and there was a trace of bitterness in her voice.

Sigrid headed for safer ground. "Exactly what happened yesterday?"

Sue Montrose fumbled in her pocket and brought out an opened pack of cigarettes of the same brand that had been found in the Bitzer apartment. She lit one with a butane lighter and inhaled deeply before answering.

"I met Julie about four and a half years ago. We worked in the same building and used to run into each other in the cafeteria down the street. She wasn't somebody you could get close to, but we'd take coffee breaks together or go shopping on our lunch hour once in a while. When she was getting married, she said something about how much trouble they were having finding a good place to live. I knew about a vacancy in my uncles' building, so I told her about it. In return, she asked me if I wanted her job at Landau and Maas Electronics when she left to have the baby. It paid fifty a week more than I was getting downstairs and was a smaller company, easier to work for, so I said yes and she recommended me.

"She and George had been seeing each other before she met Karl Redmond, but I didn't think it'd been anything serious. Then last year, she started dropping in, flirting with George, inviting him for drinks after work. He pretended he didn't want to go, but he went.

"It was none of my business," she said carefully. "He and I had only seen each other once or twice outside the office. I didn't have any strings on him. They seemed to be picking up where they left off. Julie divorced Karl and then, all of a sudden, nothing."

"Nothing?"

"She stopped coming, he stopped going."

"So you and he—?" Sigrid probed delicately.

Sue Montrose studied the drifting smoke of her cigarette. "So he and I," she agreed. "Until this past month. I thought they were starting again. She was phoning him. I found a note on the floor under his desk. He said they weren't, but he's never available on Saturday morning and—and—"

"And you wanted to find out if he was seeing Mrs. Redmond instead of his dentist?" asked Sigrid.

Sue Montrose nodded but was pricked by silent fear, wondering if the lieutenant's remark was casual or if she'd noticed George's hesitation.

"And was he?" asked the lieutenant.

"No, of course not!"

Although the sun overhead was so warm that Sigrid wished she had picked a bench in the shade, Sue Montrose shivered inside her white cardigan. Of course, she was wearing a short tennis dress and her freckled legs were bare, but Sigrid suspected the shiver came more from her questions than from physical cold.

"How long were you in apartment 3-A?" she asked, taking a small leather notebook from her shoulder bag.

"I got there around a quarter to nine. I told my uncles that I thought Julie was selling industrial secrets. They knew she'd worked for Landau and Maas before me and they believed it. They didn't like her anyhow. She was a fault-finder and demanding; a poor tipper, too, so they went along with it when I asked to use the empty apartment. And you might as well know it: I was there last Saturday, also. A bust, though. Nobody came all morning except the people in 3-B, who took Timmy somewhere.

"Julie went shopping. I followed her through Ohrbach's and Altman's and when she went into a hairdresser's after lunch, I came home."

"But yesterday?" asked Sigrid, sensing the girl's reluctance to focus on that period.

Sue Montrose dropped her cigarette on the path, crushed it with her sneakered foot, and immediately lit another. Sigrid waited patiently.

"Yesterday morning," she said at last. "I was there for over an hour before a single thing happened. At ten-fifteen, the woman from 3-B rang Julie's bell. Julie answered it and let the woman in. About five minutes later, somebody came up on the elevator, a man, and I heard the maid in 3-B let him in there. Five or ten minutes after that, the Italian lady came out with the little boy. They told Julie goodbye and then they took the elevator down.

"Nobody else visited Julie until just after twelve, when some man I've never seen before came up on the elevator and rang her bell. She didn't come to the door, but it must have been unlocked because he walked right in. He was there about ten minutes and then, instead of coming out of the front door and taking the elevator down, he sneaked out the back door and down the stairs."

A ragged flock of pigeons waddled past their bench herded by an unsteady toddler in red corduroy overalls. Her parents followed with the empty stroller and indulgent smiles.

"What happened next?" Sigrid asked.

"I thought maybe Julie had gone out. I wasn't at the door every single minute, you see. She could have left without my knowing. I thought maybe the guy had been a thief, so I went over. The door wasn't shut tight—I just touched it and it opened. Inside, there were papers all over the floor around her desk."

The girl dropped her cigarette, stuffed her hands into her sweater pockets, and very carefully placed her feet together with the toes extended as far as possible, sinking down into the bench until her body was a straight line that touched the bench only at neck and hips. Her voice became expressionless as she continued.

"I called her name in case she was there. I was going to pretend I had just dropped in while visiting my uncles. But there was no answer; and when I got to the kitchen, there she was. Lying on the floor. I thought maybe that guy had knocked her out, but then I touched her and her arms were cold and I knew she was dead."

Sigrid looked at the rough notes she'd taken and frowned. "She was cool to the touch?"

Sue Montrose nodded.

"I don't mean to belabor the point, Miss Montrose, but you entered immediately after the man left? A man who was only there ten minutes at the most?"

Again the girl nodded.

"And you're quite sure her flesh was already cool?"

"She was cold," Montrose repeated, and swallowed hard.

"You say you were away from the door at times. Can you be more specific?"

"I was there from nine till about eleven-fifteen, when I went to the kitchen for a glass of milk. I guess that took about two minutes. Then I'm afraid I dozed off for a few minutes around eleven-thirty." Her smile was rueful. "Stakeouts are pretty boring, aren't they?"

Sigrid nodded. "They can be. Did you sleep long?"

"No more than eight or ten minutes at the most. I honestly don't think anybody could have gotten past without me seeing them. I really needed a cigarette to keep me awake, but I'd left my matches in the kitchen and I thought as long as I was going, I might as well get a sandwich and go to the bathroom, too. That took exactly eight minutes, because I timed myself: from eleven fifty-five till twelve-oh-three. The man came almost immediately after I got back."

Sigrid flipped back to earlier notes and found Vico Cavatori's account of Karl Redmond's visit. "Are you sure no one else crossed the vestibule that morning?"

"Not to Julie's apartment. And not to 3-C where the old lady lives alone either. But like I said, some man came to 3-B. I couldn't see that part of the landing, but I heard him saying goodbye when he left around eleven."

"You're positive the man who left at eleven didn't go across and enter the Redmond apartment?"

"Sure. He got on the elevator and left. I never saw him and I had my eye on the peephole all the time. Someone else came out of 3-B about fifteen minutes later and that's when I went for milk."

Vico Cavatori, thought Sigrid. "Could *he* have visited Mrs. Redmond?"

"No, I waited until I heard the elevator going down before I left the door."

"Did you ever meet Julie Redmond's brother, Mickey Novak?"

Sue Montrose shook her head; but when Sigrid asked her to describe the man she'd seen enter the Redmond apartment, the details tallied with the description of Novak.

Sigrid went back over each point, but the young secretary would add nothing further—those were the times and those were the people. No one else.

Yet Sigrid could not help feeling that Miss Montrose was holding something back. She kept her pen poised for the address of the electronics firm where she worked for Franklin. "I'll have your statement typed up and someone will be around tomorrow for you to sign it, if that's convenient?"

"Okay." Sue nodded. She gathered up her racket and tennis balls, suddenly anxious to be gone. When the lieutenant offered to drop her off at her apartment, she shook her head. "It's only a ten-minute walk."

She hurried away, cutting across a grassy field, knowing the policewoman's cool gray eyes were watching her speculatively, but she couldn't help it. She needed time alone. Time to decide what to tell George. She thought about those gaps in her vigil yesterday morning and wished she hadn't told Lieutenant Harald about them.

The ten-minute walk stretched to twenty. She moved unseeingly through Sunday strollers, pausing mechanically at the corners for red lights, moving on with the crowds when the lights turned green.

As she unlocked the door of her apartment, George sprang up from the couch where he'd been watching the Mets on television with halfhearted interest.

"I was beginning to think I was going to have to post bail for you!" He smiled, moving confidently to take her in his arms.

His glass was nearly empty and not for the first time,

Sue guessed. She saw the bottle sitting on the coffee table and remembered that Jenny had a date this afternoon. She'd probably told George to help himself and George had.

Drowning his sorrows over Julie's death or giving himself Dutch courage? Suddenly angry, she wrenched free of his hold. To hell with tact, she thought.

"Where were you yesterday, George? And don't say dentist. You aren't due for a checkup till July and you had a notice from Dr. Jordils last month that his office would be closed the first three weeks of May."

George Franklin stared at her blankly.

CHAPTER 15

After finishing with Sue Montrose, Sigrid strolled back to a hotdog stand. The mustard was spicy, the sauerkraut nicely flecked with caraway seeds, and Sigrid munched contentedly while watching the end of the croquet game she'd passed earlier.

Her peripatetic lunch over, she had dialed the Redmond apartment and, getting no answer, played a hunch and stopped by headquarters, where she found Tillie letting his fingers do some of the footwork.

He described to her the custom-made key Eliza Fitzpatrick said Julie Redmond had constantly worn and told her how that had made him take a closer look at Redmond's bank statements. Sure enough, there had been periodic deductions for rental fees on a safety-deposit box. He had already set in train the necessary paperwork to allow them to open the box the next day. "And I thought you might want somebody posted there first thing tomorrow in case anybody shows up with the key?"

"It will probably be her brother," Sigrid said. "Has he been located yet?"

"Nope. I put someone on it last night, but Novak moved out of his boardinghouse around three yesterday. No forwarding address, naturally, so we've got an APB out on him. Did the Dorritt niece give you anything?"

"Yes, indeed." Sigrid described George Franklin, then reconstructed Sue Montrose's Saturday morning vigil for Tillie, who drew up another of those timetables so dear to his heart:

8:45—Sue Montrose to 3-A
10:15—Mrs. Cavatori to 3-D
10:20—Karl Redmond to 3-B
10:29—Mrs. C. and Timmy leave 3-D
11:00—Redmond leaves 3-B
11:15—Mr. C. leaves 3-B
11:15–11:17—Sue M. away from door for milk
11:28–11:40—Sue M. asleep
11:30–1:00—Gilchrist to lunch. Wet paint walked through
11:55–12:03—Sue M. away from door for lunch
12:02—Manny Dorritt sees Mickey Novak enter building
12:04—Novak to 3-D
12:15—Novak leaves via stairs
12:16—Sue M. to 3-D, finds Julie R. dead
1:15—Miss Fitzpatrick discovers body

"If Montrose and Julie Redmond were involved with the same man, maybe she was the one Miss Fitzpatrick heard Redmond yell at," Tillie suggested. "Montrose says she was getting milk at eleven-fifteen, but what if she went over to Redmond's apartment instead? That could be Miss Fitzpatrick's midmorning."

"I don't know, Tillie. I could see her going there and arguing, but then to return and continue her watch from 3-A? It doesn't seem logical."

Tillie looked dubious, knowing that murderers were not always logical.

"Besides, Cohen said the blow was delivered by a right-

handed person. Sue Montrose plays tennis and lights cigarettes with her left hand."

"Speaking of Cohen," Tillie remembered, "his report
came through a few minutes ago."

He moved the papers on his desk and handed the autopsy
findings to Sigrid.

It was a straightforward report with no surprises. Cohen
had listed the time of death as occurring between nine-
thirty and twelve-fifteen, evidently forgetting that they'd
told him Redmond had been seen alive at ten-thirty by
Mrs. Cavatori and Timmy.

"Which Sue Montrose confirms," said Sigrid. "She
heard Timmy say goodbye to his mother just as he told
us."

"And she's sure Redmond was already cool to the touch
when she went in right behind Novak?" asked Tillie. His
brow furrowed as he tried to fit it all together.

Sigrid nodded. "That would narrow down the time of
death to between ten-thirty and no later than eleven forty-
five."

"And Montrose was away from the door at least twice
during that very period."

"So she says."

Tillie looked up from his timetable. "You think she's
shielding somebody? One of her uncles?"

"Or George Franklin. He claimed he had a dental appointment yesterday morning. Sounded like a spur-of-the-
moment invention to me, and I don't think Montrose
believed it either. She sent him away before she'd talk to
me."

Sigrid turned her pen thoughtfully through slender fingers. "Try to have her statement typed up for signing by
tomorrow, Tillie, and we'll take it around to Landau and
Maas ourselves. We'll also take a copy of that telephone
tape; see if it can loosen Franklin's tongue."

"Too bad the time doesn't fit for Mickey Novak," said
Tillie. "I checked his priors: criminal mischief, second-
degree assault, burglary-two, criminal possession of a
weapon—he seemed to be building up to the big one."

He tapped the notations carrying Karl Redmond's name

and said, "Maybe we'll get the ex-husband though. I've got Jim Lowry chasing down the cabbie who's supposed to have picked him up at eleven-oh-five. Maybe we'll find he only took Redmond around the block."

Sigrid looked through the timetable again, her gray eyes calculative. "At an absolute minimum, Tillie, how long would it take someone to cross that vestibule, enter Redmond's apartment and get out again? A minute? Two minutes?"

"If he just walked in, bopped her on the head, and came straight out again?"

She nodded.

"Probably no more than ninety seconds flat. Of course, that's if she just sat there and let it happen. Wouldn't she be on her guard if someone walked straight in like that?"

"Not if it were someone she'd never had reason to fear."

"Like George Franklin?"

"Perhaps," said Sigrid, not ready to voice the unlikely notion that had occurred to her. "Franklin did know about the tap. He might even have installed it. As an executive at Landau and Maas Electronics, he must have some practical knowledge in the field. I wonder how long that thing was in place?"

"And why?" mused Tillie. "If it was for blackmail, no payments show up in her bank records. At least not in the last twelve to fourteen months."

"Does that mean you found something earlier?"

Even with the heat off, the office was warm. Wishing she could open her window, Sigrid rolled up the sleeves of her white shirt before giving her attention to the extract of Julie Redmond's bank records which Tillie had prepared.

"The Redmonds were married almost four years ago," said Tillie. "At that time, they opened a joint checking account as well as a joint savings account. But she had another savings account in her name alone in a different bank and she seems to have deposited all her paychecks in it in addition to other occasional small amounts—probably money left over from household expenses that he gave her."

"What's yours is ours; what's mine is mine alone?" asked Sigrid.

"Seems that way."

"A rather mean-spirited approach to marriage," she observed.

"Those deposits stop when she quit her job to have the little boy. Less than three years ago. But almost immediately, something new picks up."

He pointed to a list of deposits for the fifteenth of each month. They began the month before Timmy's birth and continued until fourteen months ago. Twenty-one monthly deposits of three hundred dollars each.

"Not an allowance from her husband?" asked Sigrid.

"Nope. Everything about the joint accounts remains the same," said Tillie. "Karl Redmond seems to have gradually drawn larger salaries from his father's jewelry store—about what you'd expect—but that stopped when the old man was killed. And of course, she filed for divorce the month after that, so—"

His words broke off and he frowned, struck by a sudden coincidence. "I wonder—"

He picked up one of the steno notebooks that contained his raw notes and started flipping through it. Sigrid waited patiently. She knew from experience that whatever he was looking for would eventually be found. Tillie thrived on details and she had benefited from his methodical nature too often to call him on it.

At last he thumped a lined page with pleasure. "Here it is and I was right! Old Mr. Redmond was killed on the thirteenth of that month and there were no more three-hundred-dollar deposits after that. My God! She was blackmailing her own father-in-law!"

Sigrid was less willing to jump to such an extraordinary conclusion. "If he's the source of the money, isn't it reasonable to assume it was more in the nature of a gift, freely given, because she'd borne him a grandson?"

Deflated, Tillie looked back at his dates. He found an arguing point. "But they start the month *before* Timmy was born. Besides, his present for the kid came three days after the birth. He started a college fund for Timmy with five thousand dollars as the first deposit."

"Nevertheless," Sigrid said firmly.

"Okay." For the moment, Tillie let the point pass because there was something else.

"Right after Karl Redmond moved out, she deposited seventy-five thousand in that account. And don't ask if it had something to do with a divorce settlement," he warned, "because she'd already cleaned him out good—drew everything from their joint accounts and transferred it over to her private account the day before she kicked him out of the apartment."

It was not a very nice picture that they were getting of Julie Redmond, Sigrid reflected. She knew that many marriages did end with similar money-grabbing tactics. If a union turns bitter, it may be hard to remember fairness and decency.

On the other hand, she thought, a separate savings account from the very beginning doesn't exactly argue for mutual trust and mutual sharing. In this day and age it was probably naïve to censure a woman who leaves the wedding altar after pledging to merge her life with her husband's and then heads for the nearest bank, where she coolly arranges to keep her money separate. Nevertheless . . .

Sigrid sighed and turned back to Tillie, who was explaining that the first seventy-five thousand dollars had not remained alone long. Another fifty thousand dollars had appeared six months later.

Except for an unexplained draft of thirty thousand dollars soon after the account was opened, Julie Redmond seemed to have withdrawn only a modest two or three thousand of it at a time, which she transferred to her checking account along with the monthly five hundred her ex-husband Karl contributed for child support. This had been used for day-to-day expenses. Her only extravagance seemed to be occasional splurges for clothing or a piece of furniture. Otherwise, she was not a spendthrift.

According to the last bank statement, her savings account had totaled well over a hundred thousand dollars when she was killed. With annual interest, it would have lasted several years at the rate she was spending.

"But where did it all come from?" Sigrid asked Tillie.

He threw up his hands. "I can't figure it. Sometimes she made little notes to herself on the back of her deposit slips, but not with those two."

"Any notes with those three-hundred-dollar deposits?"

"I haven't sorted out all the slips yet; but with our luck, she won't have left us anything." Tillie sounded momentarily discouraged.

Sigrid relented. "I'm no believer in coincidences," she reminded him, "but it just might be a coincidence that the payments stopped when the elder Redmond died. On the other hand, what if she knew a secret someone was paying her to keep from the old man?"

"So that when he died, they didn't have to go on paying? An employee maybe?"

"Worth looking into," she suggested.

"I'll start Peters on it." He jotted down a few quick notes to himself and then cleared everything neatly away into separate file folders. Tillie seldom punched out the minute his shift ended on weekdays, but weekends revolved around his family.

"Marian's mother's expecting us over," he explained, "and her Sunday night suppers are really something!"

He went away to brief Peters before leaving.

When he had gone, Sigrid tidied up a few loose ends on her own desk. None of the paperwork demanded immediate attention; but unlike Tillie, she had no one waiting for her except a trio of swallowtail larvae. Hardly an inducement to hurry home.

As she picked up her shoulder bag, its weight suggested an alternative, and she thought, well, why not? It had been a couple of months since she'd done any target practice and there was a firing range in the basement.

Downstairs, Sigrid signed for several rounds of ammunition, picked up a sheaf of paper targets, and headed for a far lane. Except for a uniformed patrolman who was unhappily evaluating his misses, she had the place to herself.

It always reminded her of a bowling alley—the separate lanes, each person concentrating on his own efforts, the noise. She adjusted the lightweight plastic ear mufflers, which deadened the gunshots, clipped her first target on the overhead line, and sent it down toward the end of her lane, halting it at twenty-five feet.

The police academy's advance silhouette was a black line drawing on buff paper. It was the same unsophisticated depiction of a classic bad guy as might be found in any comic strip and gave a full frontal view of a stocky man, cut off at beefy thighs, who stood slightly crouched as he squinted down the barrel of a black revolver.

There was nothing very subtle about the drawing. It was life-sized and was meant to hammer home the fact that target practice was more than a pleasant diversion or an exercise in hitting the center of concentric circles.

Sigrid brought her .38 up in a two-handed grip and steadily emptied the six chambers.

She retrieved the target sheet. Her first bullet had gone through the figure's left ear, the second through his right shoulder. The remaining four could be covered by a fifty-cent piece over the black revolver.

She reloaded, clipped a fresh target to the line, and gave it an extra twenty feet. The gun's two-inch barrel was less accurate at much distance; but again, all her shots hit the hand and gun. She kept the same range on the next two and began trying for spots precisely placed elsewhere on the target.

She was one of the lucky ones, Sigrid thought, as the bullets exploded from her gun. She'd never had to shoot at a living, breathing target. She thought she could if it became necessary. She hoped she wouldn't hesitate—good men lost their lives when their colleagues froze—but she knew deep down that if offered even the slenderest choice, she would shoot to incapacitate, not kill.

She fired a final volley, then pulled off the mufflers and gathered up the targets. As she turned to leave the range, she was startled to see Captain McKinnon watching from behind the soundproof glass. He met her as she came through the door, his hand outstretched.

"May I?" he said. It was more a command than a request. Wordlessly, she handed over the yellow paper targets.

She had worked under McKinnon for over a year now

and she still felt uncomfortable when going one-on-one with him. She'd been cursed with a tongue-tied awkwardness from childhood, but it usually subsided with familiarity. This big, rumpled man made her uneasy and she hadn't decided why. His brown eyes were sleepy-looking, but she knew they didn't miss a trick and she had often noticed a vague air of expectation when he looked at her that was absent when he turned his attention to the others.

"Not bad," he said of the first two or three targets. He shook out the last couple and asked, "What happened here?"

"They went where I wanted them to go," she said stiffly.

"You'd like it better if we gave you full-length targets to hang up so you could practice shooting for the feet or legs?" he growled. "Grow up, Harald! If you ever have to fire your gun for real, you'll be damned grateful for something as thick as a torso to aim for. And even that will seem too small at times. If your—"

McKinnon caught himself. Too late now to change the decision he'd made when this tall, grave-eyed young woman first joined his department. He'd thought then that her coolness was hostility at being assigned to the man who'd been her father's partner. The man who had walked away from that rundown hotel unscathed while her father was carried out on a stretcher with three bullets in his body.

Leif Harald had been taller than his daughter, a blond blue-eyed Viking who had smiled at Mac's caution and had thought—quite correctly, too—that their quarry was a scared little sewer rat caught up in something too big to handle. Confident, laughing Leif had forgotten that even the most cowardly rat will fight if too hopelessly cornered.

Sigrid had been such a young child then, hardly more than a baby, a toddler with enormous gray eyes whom he'd dandled on his knee and bought birthday presents for and whom he'd never seen again after Leif's funeral until the day she was assigned to him over a year ago.

McKinnon soon realized that Anne and Leif's daughter remembered nothing about that long-ago partnership; that even though Anne blamed him for Leif's death, she had not filled the girl's childhood with hate; but by then it was too late. The pattern of their working relationship was set. Besides, it was obvious that this policewoman would have resented thinking she got special treatment because of who her parents were. She was already touchy enough about her position in the department. If she ever suspected the truth, she'd probably demand a transfer and, without analyzing why, he knew that he wanted her to stay.

So let it be, he'd told himself. Forget about Leif, forget about Anne. Keep it impersonal and professional. Never mind the might-have-beens.

He thrust the targets back at Sigrid and stomped away.

If my what? wondered Sigrid. Why did McKinnon always leave her with a feeling of unspoken sentences?

CHAPTER 16

Before the branch bank that handled Julie Redmond's finances could open for business Monday morning, Detective Tildon and his two companions had talked their way past the guard at the front door and had been directed to the proper vice-president.

Mrs. Schatel was pleasantly fiftyish; she was allowing her short blond hair to go gray naturally, and the jacket of her softly tailored burgundy suit was comfortably loose. Despite her easygoing appearance, however, she was as mulishly suspicious as any other bank official that Detective Tildon had ever encountered.

"No one may open Mrs. Redmond's box without a court order," she repeated.

Patiently, Tillie started over again. "We're getting a court order," he explained.

"*And* someone from the Internal Revenue Service," said Mrs. Schatel.

"And someone from IRS," Tillie agreed. "But that's scheduled for this afternoon, Mrs. Schatel. Right now, all we're asking is to let us post two plainclothes officers here at the bank so that if anyone asks for Mrs. Redmond's box, you can point him out to them."

"But I'm trying to tell you, Detective Tildon, no one can even enter the vault area unless the owner has authorized a proxy, whose signature must be on record," said Mrs. Schatel, "and Mrs. Redmond never filed such an authorization."

"We only want to see if someone *tries*," Tillie reiterated.

"Very well," said Mrs. Schatel. "It is this bank's policy to cooperate with the police whenever possible. We can't allow any disturbance though."

Her last remark was directed at Officers Jim Lowry and Elaine Albee, who had been picked because they could look like an upwardly mobile young couple seeking a mortgage loan.

Albee smiled reassuringly, and Mrs. Schatel unbent enough to show them a couch near the loan department where they could wait and watch unobtrusively.

When Tillie returned to the office, he found Lieutenant Harald at the tag end of a telephone conversation. She saw him standing in her open doorway and motioned for him to come in.

"If you do hear from her, please have her call me," he heard her say. She enunciated her name and telephone number carefully and hung up with a slight frown.

"I can't seem to put my hands on Sue Montrose," she complained. "The receptionist at Landau and Maas says she didn't come to work this morning. That was her roommate, Jenny Wills, who said she hadn't seen Montrose since she left to play tennis with George Franklin yesterday afternoon. She said Franklin came back alone—that was when I was questioning her at the tennis courts—and she went out before Montrose returned. When she got in last night, neither Montrose nor Franklin was there. She's concerned because this is the first time Montrose has stayed out all night without leaving word."

"Did you talk to Franklin?" asked Tillie.

"Not yet. Round up a cassette player for that tape we

found, Tillie, and let's go hear what he says when we play it for him."

"*Why do you keep bringing it up? What's the point of—? Damn! Are you taping this?*"

George Franklin's darkly handsome face was wary as Julie Redmond's taped laughter filled his large, comfortably appointed office.

"Shall I play it again?" asked Sigrid, pressing the rewind button.

"No!" he said. His hand darted to his thick black hair. He smoothed it back in a gentle patting motion, then straightened his impeccable tie.

Sigrid and Tillie could see him visibly brace himself to brazen it out.

"So we once had something going," Franklin said. He paused and gave her a boyish grin. "So what? It wasn't a secret at the time. Besides, that was four years ago, as you just heard. That's when Julie decided a jeweler made better husband material than an electronics systems analyst."

"Why did you install a telephone tap for her?" asked Sigrid.

"What are friends for?" he parried lightly, but his charms weren't thawing this iceberg of a police lieutenant. He tried a different tack. Openness usually melted them.

"Look, Lieutenant Harald, I knew it wasn't strictly kosher, but Julie was an old friend and she was caught in a bad marriage. Her husband was cheating on her and she asked me to help her get the proof."

"So you accommodated out of friendship, pure and simple?"

He nodded.

"And not because she held something over you?" The woman's tone was so icy that he shivered involuntarily and reminded himself that there was no way she could know what Julie had known.

"What mistake had you made that you didn't want her to keep bringing up?"

Franklin's wariness returned. "Now, Lieutenant," he said urbanely, "as Julie said, we all make mistakes and we make them all the time. I don't know which particular mistake Julie had in mind—maybe that I let her get away? Whatever it was, it certainly can't have anything to do with her death."

"Where were you Saturday morning?"

"I had a dental appointment."

"His name and address?" Tillie asked, his pencil poised.

Franklin's urbanity turned to alarm. "What do you need that for?"

"To verify your alibi," Sigrid answered.

"*Alibi?* What the hell do I need—? You think *I* killed Julie?"

"If you were at your dentist's, it would prove you didn't," she said.

"Ask Sue. She was there, wasn't she? She'll tell you I didn't come near Julie's apartment Saturday morning."

"Where *is* Miss Montrose?" asked Sigrid, who had noticed the empty desk outside when they came in.

He shrugged. "Home, I guess. We had a fight yesterday—well, not a fight really, more of a misunderstanding—and I guess she's still mad. She didn't come in today."

"Her roommate says she didn't come home last night either. In fact, Mr. Franklin, she seems to be missing, and you were the last one to see her. And now you say you fought? What about?"

"To hell with this!" cried Franklin. "I'm not saying another word till I see my lawyer, and you can't make me!"

He pushed back his padded leather chair, stood up, and belligerently put his hands on his hips.

Sigrid stood just as abruptly. "Very well, Mr. Franklin. Shall we say three o'clock in my office at headquarters?"

Tillie cleared his throat. "You're scheduled to be at the bank at two," he reminded her.

"So I am," she agreed, and told Franklin, "Change that to three-thirty instead."

His bluff called, Franklin looked back at her numbly.

"Don't forget the information about your dentist," Sigrid said. "And, Mr. Franklin?"

"Yes?"

"Don't make us have to send an officer with an arrest warrant," she said kindly. "Be there."

As she and Tillie left his office, George Franklin bent over his telephone and began dialing.

At the branch bank near East Seventy-sixth Street, Jim Lowry nudged his colleague. "What do you think, Lainey?"

Elaine Albee casually lifted her blue eyes from the current issue of *Working Woman* and let them drift over the noon-time surge of customers who'd just entered the bank. Almost immediately she saw the slender, dark-haired man Lowry must have meant. They'd both studied Mickey Novak's mug shots and description very carefully; this man was a perfect match.

In accordance to the plan they'd agreed upon, Lowry rose and made his way toward the newcomer, who had joined the shortest line. He was right behind him when the man inquired about visiting a safe deposit box.

"That's Mrs. Schatel," caroled the young teller. "First desk on the left."

Elaine Albee pulled out her compact and busied herself with a lip moistener as the dark-haired young man approached Mrs. Schatel's desk.

"May I help you?" the bank official asked.

"My sister asked me to get something out of her box for her," he mumbled.

For all her earlier objections, Mrs. Schatel's voice was calm and pleasant as she reached for her card file. "Certainly," she said. "What is your sister's name?"

"J-Julie Redmond," he said nervously. "Mrs. Julie Redmond."

"You *do* have the key?" she asked.

A flash of gold gleamed in the man's hand.

"I'll take that, Novak," said Jim Lowry from just above his right ear.

Mickey Novak whirled and, without hesitating for an instant, kneed Lowry in the groin with such viciousness that the young policeman dropped to the floor in excruciating pain.

Elaine Albee leaped over her partner's writhing body and darted after Novak, who eeled through the startled customers and was out the door before the guard could intercept him. Just past the main entrance, a postman's cart blocked his path for a fraction and Albee hurtled through the doors after him.

Novak's foot slipped on a candy wrapper someone had discarded on the sidewalk and, as he regained his balance, Elaine Albee made a flying tackle and pinned his left leg. Both crashed to the ground, Novak twisted sharply, and the toe of his right shoe connected with her left jaw.

As pain exploded through her head, her hands went limp and Mickey Novak wriggled free. By the time her head cleared and she was on her feet again, excited bystanders could only point to the general direction in which he'd fled.

"Unbloody, but bruised and bowed," Tillie reported as he reentered Sigrid's office with a fresh ice pack. "The doctor says Lowry won't be back to work for at least three or four days."

Sigrid sighed and turned back to Elaine Albee, who took the ice pack gratefully and held it to her swollen jaw. The skin wasn't broken but it looked raw and tight and was already exhibiting a range of color from bright red to blue-black.

"I feel so stupid!" said the girl. "I had your murderer on the ground and then I let him get away."

"You were on the ground, too," Sigrid pointed out. "Don't heap ashes on your head, Albee. It could have happened to anyone. And if it's any consolation, I rather doubt that he's his sister's killer."

She carefully hid from the younger woman the disappointment she felt. Albee was a good officer and would get better with more seasoning, but it had been a letdown to return to headquarters feeling that everything was starting to fall into place only to learn that one of her stakeout officers was in the hospital and the other probably should be.

"I'm okay, Lieutenant, really," Albee insisted. "The

doctor said there was no fracture and he gave me a needleful of some sort of enzyme derivative that's supposed to dissolve this bruise in a few days. At least we got this."

She held out her hand and a golden filigreed heart and key dangled from the delicate chain. "Novak dropped it when Jim surprised him."

"Bingo!" said Tillie. "The Fitzpatrick kid was right."

"Very nice," Sigrid agreed, taking the chain. "Anything else, Albee?"

"No, Lieutenant." Elaine Albee shook her head and the unguarded movement made her wince with pain.

"Then take the rest of the day off," Sigrid said. "And no false heroics," she added crisply as the girl started to object. "You've earned it."

One of her rare smiles softened the command, and Elaine Albee left the office revising an opinion formed when she first joined the department four months earlier.

Maybe the lieutenant wasn't a cast-iron robot after all.

CHAPTER 17

As no will had been found among Julie Redmond's papers, it was assumed that her son Timmy would be declared sole heir. Accordingly, Vico Cavatori's attorney had spoken to Karl Redmond's, and between them someone from a third firm had been commissioned to look after the child's interests, a Mr. Hagstrom.

He arrived at the bank promptly at two and introduced himself to Sigrid and Tillie. He had met Mr. Pinchelli from the Internal Revenue Service before.

Mrs. Schatel forebore to complain about the morning's disturbance and graciously showed them into the vault area. She was pleased to see that Julie Redmond's key had been recovered. Without it, they would have had to open the box by force and such destruction went against the bank officer's orderly soul.

It was a silent ceremony: Mrs. Schatel inserted the bank's key, Mr. Hagstrom turned the filigreed copy Julie Redmond had worn around her neck when she was killed; then they adjourned with the box to a small private cubicle where Mrs. Schatel left them without showing any sign of unprofessional curiosity.

Mr. Hagstrom lifted the metal lid and found an unsealed manila envelope. "Well, well, well," he said softly, spilling its contents on the bare table.

"Yes, indeed," said Mr. Pinchelli and helped him count the stacks of bills. They were mostly hundreds with several packs of fifties and totaled an astonishing eighty thousand dollars.

After the envelope came a small washleather pouch, and somehow Sigrid found herself unsurprised by the sight of those glittering, flashing stones. Most were small faceted diamonds, but there were several sapphires and the fiery green blaze of emeralds.

"These will have to be appraised," said Mr. Pinchelli disapprovingly, and Mr. Hagstrom nodded in agreement.

"Add the hundred and twenty-five thousand she deposited in her savings account this past year to that eighty thousand you just found, subtract the total from half a million, and you'll probably be close," Sigrid told them.

"Is half a million a guess, Lieutenant, or specific knowledge?" asked the IRS man courteously.

"Her father-in-law was killed last spring while carrying a quantity of unset stones which were not recovered. Their estimated worth was set at half a million."

"Before you claim these as stolen property," said Mr. Hagstrom, "I must remind you that it is very difficult to prove the provenance of unset stones."

"Does it matter?" asked Sigrid. "I think Timmy and his father were the elder Mr. Redmond's only near kin, so it all amounts to the same thing, doesn't it?"

"Only if the boy remains with his father," said Mr. Hagstrom cryptically.

Sigrid shrugged. Other authorities could haggle about ownership of the gems; now that she had seen them, their disposition didn't really concern her. What did hold her interest was the remaining item in the steel box—a ninety-minute cassette tape.

"It might record financial information," objected Mr. Pinchelli.

"I shall want a signed receipt for that tape and a notarized transcript as soon as possible," chimed in Mr. Hagstrom.

"Of course," Sigrid said noncommittally.

Each of the three made an identifying mark on the cassette's plastic casing, and Tillie provided an envelope in which to carry it back to headquarters.

"What about the necklace?" asked Mr. Hagstrom as he watched her return it to her shoulder bag. "I'm afraid we'll have to hang on to that for now," said Sigrid. "It's part of our investigation."

They exchanged receipts all around; then Tillie and Sigrid departed, leaving Mr. Hagstrom and Mr. Pinchelli doing an Alphonse/Gaston over whose gemologist should appraise the jewels they'd found.

The tape began with the buzz of a telephone bell heard through the receiver. A man's voice answered. "*Yeah?*"

"*Mickey? Julie. Want to go with me next week to buy that new carpet I was telling you about?*"

"*Huh?*"

"*You remember, Mickey—the cream-colored carpet I wanted for the living room?*"

"*Oh yeah, that silk thing that costs an arm and a leg. Where you gonna get the money for it?*"

"*Maybe I'll have the money next week,*" she said archly. "*Karl's father is supposed to make a large sale tomorrow and Karl thinks he might get an extra bonus.*"

"*This is it, Julie?*" Novak's voice squeaked with excitement. Julie's voice, on the other hand, lacked his spontaneity. It was almost as if she were reading a script.

"*He's taking a consignment of jewels over to the Hilton for some rich Arab to look at. Can you believe it? He'll just grab a taxi near the shop sometime after lunch with half a million dollars' worth of diamonds in his pocket like they were marbles. No guards, no nothing. Crazy, isn't it? I hope no one tries to rob him.*"

"*Maybe I'll go along and be his bodyguard,*" laughed Novak. "*Tomorrow after lunch, huh?*"

There were clicking sounds on the tape and several inches unwound with nothing on it except static. Tillie leaned over to touch the fast forward button when an abrupt click signaled a new conversation.

"—*oon and I did it!*" crowed Novak's jubilant voice.

"*Who is this?*" asked Julie Redmond sharply.

"*What do you mean who's this? It's me. Mickey. Your brother. And I've got 'em!*"

"*Got what, Mickey?*"

If he hadn't been so excited, the artificial innocence in her voice might have alerted him.

"*The diamonds, Julie! What the hell do you think I meant? Diamonds and emeralds and some sapphires, too! God, they're pretty!*"

"*How?*"

"*I was waiting at a coffee shop down from his place from eleven-thirty on. About two o'clock, out he comes. No cabs in sight. I knew he'd go on down to the avenue, so I hurried on ahead, stepped in that alley near the corner, and when he came by, I grabbed him. He put up a fight, but I bopped him good.*"

"*Oh, my God, Mickey! What have you done? Did you hurt him?*"

"*Who cares? Now we can buy a dozen fancy rugs!*"

Another click and this time, the silence was final. Tillie rewound the tape.

"Do you want to hear it again?" he asked.

Sigrid shook her head.

"She really set him up good, didn't she?" said Tillie. "She must have talked him into letting her put the jewels in her deposit box for safety and then played him a copy of the tape."

"Nicely staged to sound as if she were just passing on careless gossip about her husband's business and that she was astounded that he'd acted on it so violently," said Sigrid.

"Do you suppose he got a penny out of it?"

"Wasn't there an unexplained thirty-thousand-dollar withdrawal soon after she opened her new savings account? Maybe that went to him."

"I'll have transcripts made," said Tillie, ejecting the tape from the player. "Want me to send a copy over to Timmy's lawyer?"

"Not just yet. We might—"

The telephone on her desk interrupted discreetly.

"Lieutenant Harald . . . Who? . . . Oh yes, Hodson." She listened quietly. "Quite right, Hodson. Thank you."

"Trouble at the Redmond apartment again?" asked Tillie.

Sigrid frowned. "Not the kind you mean. Hodson said Vico Cavatori was just carried out on a stretcher. Another heart attack."

"Dead?"

"No, but it doesn't sound good."

Once again that errant possibility niggled at Sigrid's mind. She dismissed it and turned her thoughts to the upcoming interview with George Franklin.

"Call around and see if anyone's heard from Sue Montrose yet," she told Tillie.

CHAPTER 18

The ambulance's interior was larger than it looked from outside, thought Vico Cavatori, or was that only because he was lying down?

He was very tired, yet part of his mind was oddly alert. The dark face that kept bending over his—a white jacket, red and blue striped tie—was he Spanish, Indian, or Pakistani? So many nationalities in this great city which had taken him, too, so long ago. The dark-eyed young man smiled at him encouragingly each time he bent down, but he couldn't smile back.

There was a cold, rubbery smell to the oxygen they were giving him. He had blacked out only a moment it seemed, and suddenly here he was, hurtling through Manhattan streets, the siren more muffled than he would have thought.

The pain in his chest had subsided, but it was still there, waiting.

Through half-closed eyes he saw Luisa crouched beside him, frantic with fear. She clutched the crystal rosary that had hung above Paolo's picture. Why that one? Why not the amethyst beads Pope John had blessed for them and which she had carried ever since that sunlit day in Rome?

Sunlight and the crowds cheering and car horns blowing for the blessed new Bishop of Rome. Giovanni Ventitre.

Santa Maria, how was it possible that more than twenty years had slipped away since then?

How old would Paolo be now?

Luisa's fingers told the decades, slipping along the beveled crystal beads like time across their lives, but her lips only said his name over and over. He wanted to lift his hand and pat hers comfortingly; he could not move it.

So very tired.

Sleep, the longest sleep of all would not be unwelcome. Only that it would grieve Luisa so.

Again, the old sadness swept over him, the years of knowing he was an end, not a continuance—not through him would his family's blood flow into the future.

Luisa should have had a dozen children to comfort her when he died, to distract her with grandchildren, to prove that his life went on.

At least she would not be completely alone now. There was the child. Timmy. Karl would not object. Already, he had half given his consent for them to keep the boy. Not of their blood maybe, but surely of their hearts.

Making a new life for Timmy would help Luisa into a life without him. And how good for the boy. Luisa had tried to keep from him the way Julie abused Timmy, but he had known.

He had known.

The ambulance swerved and came to an abrupt halt. The rear doors were flung open.

"Here we go," said the white-coated attendant.

CHAPTER 19

Shortly after three-thirty that afternoon, Detective Tildon rapped on Sigrid's half-open door and stuck his head in.

"Got a minute before Franklin gets here, Lieutenant?"

Sigrid looked up from her work and motioned him to a chair by her desk.

"I've been putting everything we've got in chronological order," he explained, handing her a sheet of paper, "and I was thinking about those three-hundred-dollar deposits Julie Redmond made for twenty-one months."

"Yes?"

"They started right after she quit her job to have the little boy and they end fourteen months ago."

"Just before old Mr. Redmond was killed," she nodded. "So?"

"So George Franklin told us the tap was installed to get divorce dirt on her husband, but now we know it was really to set up Mickey Novak so he'd kill her father-in-law and she'd wind up with all the jewels."

"Are you suggesting Franklin was in on that?" Sigrid asked dubiously.

"Not necessarily. She wouldn't have shared that with any more people than she'd have to, would she?"

"Well, then?"

"Well, what if it wasn't just because she was such a good friend that he put the tap on for her?"

Sigrid leaned back in her chair, elbows on the arm rests, her finger tips tented before her. It was her favorite listening position.

"Explain."

Tillie hesitated. Brilliant bursts of intuitive logic were seldom his, but this had seemed like an inevitable progression.

"You're always saying that the simplest explanation is usually the correct one," he said. "I just don't think it's a coincidence that those deposits stopped when they did. I think Julie Redmond was blackmailing George Franklin and she let him off the hook when he put the tap on her phone."

Sigrid considered his chronology. "Good point, Tillie. Certainly makes more sense that way."

Pleased, Tillie straightened his papers and glanced at his watch. "Franklin's late," he noted. "I'll be at my desk when you want me."

Sigrid picked up the report she'd been reading when a thought occurred to her. "You had Jim Lowry checking for Karl Redmond's cab. Did he have a chance to find it before Novak took him out of action this morning?"

Tillie looked stricken. "I forgot all about asking him. I'll go call now."

He returned in a few minutes and reported, "The nurse at the hospital says he's under sedation and won't be lucid before six, so I called Albee. Lowry hadn't mentioned it to her, but she said she'd follow up on it. I told her to go ahead."

"Good. You did put an APB out on Novak, didn't you?"

He nodded.

"And I suppose there's no word on Sue Montrose yet?"

"Nope. Her roommate wants to file a missing persons on her, but I told her it was too soon. What do you think?"

"Hold off another day," she decided. "It's not even

twenty-four hours yet. Maybe Franklin will remember something pertinent."

Both of them automatically checked the time. Ten to four.

George Franklin was now twenty minutes late.

By four-fifteen, they agreed that George Franklin did not intend to keep his appointment. Tillie got on the telephone and extracted as much information as the receptionist at Landau and Mass Electronics could supply: Mr. Franklin had left the office around noontime saying he didn't feel well and that he was going home. She obligingly confirmed Franklin's current home address and telephone number.

On the off chance that she might know, he asked if Franklin owned a car.

"Oh sure!" said the receptionist. "A white Volvo sedan."

He thanked her and tried the telephone number she'd provided. After twenty rings, it was apparent that no one would answer at Franklin's apartment.

A quick check with the Department of Motor Vehicles gave them a license plate number, and Tillie put it on the teletype with orders to locate and report only. Apprehending could come later.

"Nothing to do now but wait," Tillie told Sigrid on his way home. "You staying?"

"Not too long," Sigrid answered, eying the diminished pile of reports before her.

As Tillie left, he glanced back at the dark head bent over her work. Beyond the fact that she was unmarried and seemed to live alone, he knew almost nothing about the lieutenant's off-duty hours. All his life, Tillie had been surrounded by a cheerful, noisy family and he occasionally found himself wondering what it would be like to go home to silence every day.

It was very seldom that he had their row house in Brooklyn to himself, but on the few occasions that he'd come home to find Marian gone and all the kids out, he'd felt uneasy and restless until they were back again. He wondered if the lieutenant ever felt silence closing in on her.

Sigrid worked for another forty-five minutes until she came across a message slip that had somehow got mixed in with the papers on her desk. It was logged two-ten and said, "Call Jill Gill." A telephone number was included.

She dialed, waited, and had decided to hang up on the tenth ring; but a breathless voice answered on the eighth.

"I've really got to see about having an extension put in the garden," it said. "That's where I was. Just be glad I wasn't in the tub. Who's this?"

Bemused, Sigrid identified herself.

"Terrific!" cried the entomologist. "Look, I'm giving a slide talk on lepidoptera at seven-thirty tonight. Want to come? It's just a basic look at life cycles because it's mostly for kids. Prettyman Day School down in the Village."

"Could I bring a friend?" Sigrid asked, thinking that Roman Tramegra ought to hear her talk if he was really going to write about the things.

"Of course! Bring as many as you like. Bring a dozen. They never fill the hall. Parents like to see visiting experts listed on the school schedule, but they don't like toddling out themselves. We'll probably just have the science-fair types."

She rang off, promising to keep an eye out for Sigrid.

Sigrid felt a bit guilty as she hung up. Jill Gill had given her those caterpillars so enthusiastically, and here she'd foisted them off on Roman.

She dialed her mother's number, since he was still staying there. When Anne Harald found him so down-and-out in Italy and sent him home with a key to her empty apartment, she'd expected him to pull himself together and reorder his life.

Tramegra, on the other hand, had decided that an unoccupied apartment was an invitation to thieves. He had declared himself caretaker-in-residence until such time as either Anne returned or an irresistibly cheap apartment presented itself to his notice. So far, two months had gone by and he was still firmly entrenched.

"Hello-please-say?" said a thin, unfamiliar voice.

"Roman?" she asked, wondering if she'd reached a wrong number.

There was a flurry of confused sounds, then his deep bass voice filled her ear. "Roman Tramegra here."

Sigrid relayed Dr. Gill's invitation, and he fell upon it with what seemed to her excessive gratitude.

"You have saved my life!" he informed her in his solemn blend of cinema English and educated Midwest. "Your kindness is a sun to my dark despair! I shall bring supper."

Sigrid wasn't eager for him to bring back the remains of the broccoli casserole, which she had insisted he take home with him Saturday evening. She tried to express it diplomatically, but Tramegra brushed her words aside.

"There's none left," he said darkly. "I shall have to stop for something of a takeout nature. Mexican or Italian?"

"What about Chinese?" she countered.

"I shall never eat oriental food again," he snarled. "Kipling was right."

"Kipling?" asked Sigrid, wondering how Kipling had gotten into a fast food discussion.

"East is East and West is West and never the twain should meet."

CHAPTER 20

"Comforting the afflicted is all very well," said Roman Tramegra as he divided their anchovy and ripe olive pizza with magisterial exactitude, "but if you're already sheltering the homeless, you should not allow your good Samaritan impulses to run away with you."

"First come, first served?" asked Sigrid, surreptitiously removing the ripe olives, something she'd never acquired a taste for.

Roman looked at her suspiciously, ready to take offense with the first hint of amusement.

"Your mother is a dear generous woman," he said, "but she disregards the limits of what is feasible."

In short, thought Sigrid, her mother should not have thrown her apartment open to a large family of boat people while Roman was still in residence.

"I just don't understand where she met them," said Sigrid.

In her last letter, Anne Harald had written that she expected to move on to Ireland in the next week or so.

"How could she run across boat people in Ireland?"

"She didn't," Roman said gloomily. "That Stewart woman had them and she bullied Anne into housing them until she comes back. It's only supposed to be until they're assimilated. Oil and water, if you ask me. They'll never assimilate."

"*Cameron* Stewart?" asked Sigrid, beginning to see the light.

Anne Harald's circle of acquaintances was almost as varied as Oscar Nauman's, for she greeted life with wide-open arms and only the most miserable misanthrope failed to respond to her sunny nature; but Cameron Stewart was not one of her usual lame ducks.

Through hard work and a thick skin, the woman had risen high in the city's social services bureaucracy, and she was so relentlessly optimistic that she made even Anne tired. She periodically blasted the city budget's penny-pinching attitude toward its poor and needy and, when told that the city simply couldn't afford all that she asked, told them that the word *can't* ought to be banished from the city council's vocabulary. She would probably win a major humanitarian award one day if someone didn't strangle her first.

No, Cammie Stewart would see nothing awkward about sticking an anglophile with a houseful of Orientals.

"There's *nine* of them," said Roman. "Husband, wife, two grandmothers, an uncle, a sister, and three incredibly tiny children—I say, don't you want your olives?"

He took the neat pile Sigrid had collected on the edge of her plate and sprinkled them over his half of the pizza.

"They've spread sleeping mats *all* over the living room and down the hall. The uncle is camped in the vestibule, the grandmothers in the kitchen. They refuse to use Anne's room because she's their hostess. They say it isn't seemly! I ask you—is it seemly to sleep under the kitchen table?"

"But, Roman, these people are homeless. They've lost everything."

"I know, I know!" he sighed. "It sounds so pretty and self-centered to carp. I know that, my dear. And it isn't that I *mind* sharing. Do you know, I offered them some of my broccoli casserole and they flushed it down the toilet, so it isn't as if they were actually starving or anything. And then they did something perfectly *revolting* with raw fish heads!"

Sigrid sipped her wine and tried to choke back the laughter that came bubbling up at the vision Roman had conjured of West clashing head on with East.

Prettyman Day School was a modern three-story educational laboratory; but like grade schools everywhere, it smelled of chalk dust, crayons, and fresh pencil shavings, with an occasiodnal whiff of formaldehyde and Popsicles.

Despite Dr. Gill's prediction, the auditorium was nearly full. Murmuring apologies, Sigrid and Roman slipped past parents and bright-eyed children to a pair of seats halfway down a middle row.

Gill herself was being instructed in the intricacies of the school's new slide projector when they arrived, and she did not see them at first. While the principal called the meeting to order, she scanned the audience and flashed Sigrid a grin.

Her soft yellow caftan was the same shade as her Dutch bob, and her rhinestone-studded harlequin glasses glittered in the overhead lights as she responded to the principal's introduction and set the mood with some preliminary remarks. At her signal, the lights were doused and an exquisite zebra swallowtail floated onto the screen, its black and white stripes a nice contrast to the vivid red patches on its hindwings. In rapid succession, Dr. Gill snapped through a quick overview of brightly colored North American species.

"Oooh!" breathed a little boy in the seat next to Sigrid as a cloud of dainty blues hovered over a rain puddle, forever fixed in time and space.

"Now how do butterflies begin?" Jill Gill asked rhetorically.

She was an excellent showman, but, along with a nonstop humorous commentary, she managed to slip in quite a lot of technical, scientific information as the slides followed a monarch butterfly from egg to chrysalis, from adult emergence back to the laying of another egg.

Roman was entranced. If he could duplicate the crispness of these slides with the caterpillars on Sigrid's kitchen counter, surely *Today's Kid* would buy a full-length article on raising butterflies in the city. And they paid a full eight cents a word, too.

The lights came up and eager hands signaled questions. "Perhaps she'll come and have a drink with us?" said Roman, who had questions of his own but didn't want to compete with nine-year-olds.

As the meeting broke up, Sigrid and Roman walked down to the projector where Jill Gill was packing up her slides, accepting compliments from pleased parents, autographing her book on moths and butterflies, and occasionally identifying various larva or abandoned cocoons that the children thrust upon her.

"I think that's an Io caterpillar," she told a ponytailed youngster clutching a mayonnaise jar stuffed with rose leaves and a munching green worm that had spiny tufts along its back.

"Does it sting?" asked the little girl.

"It certainly does," said Dr. Gill, her eyes serious behind those preposterous turquoise glasses. "Most don't, you know, but Ios burn like nettle rash. Keep it—just don't pet it. It'll spin a cocoon soon and the moth that comes out will be a gorgeous golden brown with a large black eyespot on each hindwing."

"Will it still sting?"

"Nope."

Despite the assurance, the child looked dubiously at her catch. "Maybe I'll put it back on Daddy's rosebush," she said.

"You certainly will not!" said her mother. "Remember what Daddy told you? When you're tired of it, you must let us dispose of it."

"Young lady," said Tramegra casually, "if you don't want that caterpillar, may I have it?"

Cunning entered the girl's eyes. "Fifty cents," she said.

"Agatha!" exclaimed her mother.

"Twenty-five," Tramegra countered.

"A dollar," grinned the child.

"On second thought, fifty cents seems a reasonable

price," Tramegra said. He gave her two quarters and beamed as she handed over the mayonnaise jar.

"Have you been a collector long?" asked Dr. Gill.

They had gone to a cocktail lounge near the Prettyman Day School that leaned toward Polynesian decor. Dr. Gill was sipping something tall and green with rather a large amount of fruit in it.

Tramegra fished pineapple spears from a coconut shell of piña colada. "Only started this weekend," he admitted. "Sigrid's letting me help with the caterpillars you gave her Saturday morning."

"I can't always be there to feed them," Sigrid said lamely. Her complement of fruit was limited to the single slice of lime floating in her gin and tonic.

"You needn't make excuses," smiled Jill Gill. "It isn't easy to sidetrack Oscar when he gets a notion in his head, is it?"

She cocked her round blond head and her rhinestone glasses twinkled mischievously.

Sigrid ignored the innuendo.

"If Sigrid doesn't want the books you brought, may I borrow them?" asked Roman. "I promise you, dear lady, that I will take excellent care of them."

He had found an illustration of his new moth and wanted her opinion of when it would spin a cocoon.

"It's in its final molt—no more than two or three days."

"That long?" he asked, disappointed. "These leaves won't last past tomorrow. Now where can I borrow more, I wonder? Isn't there a rose garden in Central Park?"

"There is," said Sigrid. "Want to know what the fine for vandalism is? The park gardeners are touchy about having their bushes mauled."

"I shall be very discreet," said Roman. "They won't notice a thing."

He turned to Dr. Gill and began asking questions about children's books, publishers in general, and royalties in specific.

Embarrassed, Sigrid started to remonstrate, but Jill Gill

was so used to asking personal questions herself that she didn't seem to mind answering his.

Sigrid shrugged and signaled for another round of drinks. As she felt in her purse for her wallet, her fingers touched the letters she had scooped from her mailbox when she and Roman passed through the lobby earlier in the evening. Among the bills and circulars was another communiqué from Mrs. Jacob L. Wolfermann.

Mrs. Wolfermann was co-president of the tenants' association in Sigrid's apartment building. A tireless activist for tenants' rights, she had a vigilante's suspicious nature and spun a nebulous web of spies around the company that managed their building.

Mrs. Wolfermann had documented horror stories of landlord neglect and harassment in other buildings. Compared to them, their landlord was a model of humanity. Minor repairs might take an exasperatingly long time, but at least heat rose all winter, air was properly conditioned in the summer, and hot water flowed year-round.

Still management could change hands; humanity could evaporate. Sigrid was no joiner. She waved no banners, marched in no parades; nevertheless, she was quite willing to pay yearly dues if it encouraged people like Mrs. Wolfermann to watchdog her rights. She just wished Mrs. Wolfermann didn't feel obligated to issue status reports every few weeks. In Sigrid's opinion, no news was still the best.

With her two companions deep in conversation about press runs and copies shipped, Sigrid quietly opened the legal size envelope and read the short letter it contained. She read it again.

"Something wrong, my dear?" asked Roman.

She looked at him blankly. "My building's being converted to a co-op. The landlord is going to file a plan next week."

She handed over Mrs. Wolfermann's letter and Tramegra read it with mounting indignation. "They can't *do* this to you!" he said stoutly.

"Sure they can," said Jill. "It may take awhile but sooner or later you'll have to buy or get out."

Sigrid shuddered, remembering the periodic upheavals of her childhood. Other mothers bought new furniture or rearranged the old; Anne Harald kept the same furniture in the same arrangement and changed apartments instead. She moved at least once a year, sometimes more often.

As a child, Sigrid never knew when she would come home from school to find a rental truck parked in front of their building and some of Anne's photography students carting her bedroom furniture down the steps.

Even after all these years of living in the same apartment, seeing one of those orange and black trucks could still give her a split second of apprehension.

"I don't want to move," she said.

"Well, you certainly don't want to *buy* it," said Roman, who occasionally kept his eye on the important points. "My dear Sigrid, I don't wish to hurt your feelings, but if this Mrs. Wolfermann's information is correct, you'll pay an *exorbitant* sum for what is—forgive me, my dear—rather a mediocre apartment."

"Perhaps you won't have to do either," Jill comforted. "Your tenants' association can fight the conversion. You can appeal to the State Division of Housing and Community Renewal, take it through the appellate courts, and if that fails, letters to newspapers, picket lines, injunctions." She sounded gleeful at the prospects. "You could delay it for years!"

It sounded worse than moving, thought Sigrid.

CHAPTER 21

Sigrid's first unguarded reaction when her telephone began ringing at five Tuesday morning was that Oscar Nauman must have returned unexpectedly. No one else ever called at such an ungodly hour.

Her next reaction was to wonder briefly if something had happened to Anne. It was already midmorning in Belfast. Or did she mean midnight last night? She rather thought there was a five hours' difference, but whether New York time was earlier or later she could never remember. Neither could Anne, for that matter.

Tillie's anxious voice put an end to her speculation.

"Sorry to wake you, Lieutenant, but Peters just called me."

"It's okay, Tillie," she answered, stifling a yawn. "What did he have?"

"Suffolk County reports that George Franklin's car is parked behind a cottage in Port Jefferson."

Sigrid threw back the blanket, swung her long legs over the edge of the bed, and reached for a brush to begin untangling her mass of dark hair. "Any sign of Franklin himself?"

"Someone similar to his description was seen entering the cottage last night. They think it's still occupied."

Sigrid was silent, considering the probabilities. It was five o'clock now, and Port Jefferson was what? Sixty miles out on Long Island?

"Lieutenant?"

"If we left now, Tillie, do you think we could be there by seven?"

"This time of day? Sure."

Emerging from her apartment—her soon-to-be-a-co-op, Sigrid remembered unhappily—she found a gray morning. New Jersey's industrial fumes had drifted across the Hudson and a thin drizzle held in all the city's muggy odors without washing them away. Street traffic was light, however, and within half an hour she had checked out a car and was heading across the East River to Brooklyn.

To most native Manhattanites, the other four boroughs of the city might as well lie in the ancient mapmaker's *terra incognita*; and Sigrid held onto Tillie's instructions as to a lifeline: down Flatbush Avenue, left onto Atlantic, then straight on to the playground between Elton and Linwood, where Tillie waited for her in the family sedan.

A sleepy-eyed redhead sat behind the wheel, and she gave Sigrid a friendly smile of recognition through the rain-glazed windshield when Sigrid pulled alongside. Marian Tildon was thin and birdlike with an equable disposition and a chest even flatter than Sigrid's.

As Sigrid rolled down the window on that side, Marian called, "Lovely morning for a drive, Lieutenant."

Sigrid spared a glance at the heavy gray skies. "Lovely isn't the word I'd have chosen."

The woman's mischievous face split in a mischievous grin.

"Me neither, actually. I, for one, am going back to bed."

From the brilliant red suffusing Tillie's round face, Sigrid suspected that Marian Tildon had been told how much she disliked early morning risings. She also disliked being an object of third-party conversation, but the remark had been too good-natured to resent.

"You mind driving?" she asked Tillie, sliding into the

passenger seat. After all, Brooklyn was his territory, not hers.

Tillie circled the car. "Make him stop for coffee," Marian suggested, watching Sigrid stifle another yawn.

She gave a cheery wave as they pulled away from her.

Sigrid was not a talkative person, especially not in the early morning, and Tillie was tactful enough to respect her silence.

They drove through Brooklyn and Queens with only the steady swooshing of the windshield wipers to counterpoint the background murmur of their radio tuned to the police band. As they passed into Nassau County, Tillie pulled off the Expressway and found a coffee shop. He splashed back to the car with foam cups of hot black coffee and a couple of sugared doughnuts.

By then, Sigrid was ready for both and they munched and sipped companionably while the uninspiring housing developments slid past. Although traffic was still light in their direction, the inbound lanes were beginning to clog up. The rain slacked off as they left the eastbound Long Island Expressway and picked up the Northern State Parkway into Suffolk County.

"My father had a cousin who lived out here when he was a kid," Tillie said. "Near Huntington. He said it was all farms right up through the Second World War. Potatoes and truck farms and ducks."

The open fields had given way to bedroom communities so long ago that every lawn was overgrown with tall trees and well-established bushes; but there were still occasional stretches of woodlands and scrub tracts.

The sun broke through as they picked up the Nesconset Highway, and when Sigrid rolled down her window, she fancied she could already smell the salt air of Long Island Sound. In less than fifteen minutes, they were entering Port Jefferson.

Originally an old fishing village and still the southern terminus for the Bridgeport summer ferry from Connecticut, the town was now home port for a flotilla of pleasure boats. Luxury yachts and tall sailboats bobbed democratically in the harbor with modest outboard motorboats.

Summer sailors would soon crowd the picturesque narrow streets and rent the white-picket-fenced cottages, stroll along the harbor, or idle in and out of determinedly quaint boutiques and pubs.

It was still a week before Memorial Day and the traditional opening of the summer season, but there was a fresh-paint sense of anticipation in the air—an attractive little town all prettied up for its party guests.

Through Peters back at headquarters, Tillie had arranged to be met by one of the local police officers and they spotted his car in a bank parking lot as scheduled.

"Next week we might have missed him," said the pug-nosed officer, who looked too young to be driving a car, much less wearing a law enforcer's uniform. "Once the season starts, seems like every square foot's got a different car on it."

Driving slowly, he led them through winding lanes to a tiny white clapboard cottage with blue shutters. The walk was bordered by a line of perky red and blue petunias. In the drive behind the cottage was George Franklin's white Volvo sedan.

"Need any help?" asked their guide as Sigrid and Tillie got out of their car.

"I don't think so, thank you," answered Sigrid.

She and Tillie had so often encountered jurisdictional badgering when entering another command that they were somewhat surprised when the youth said, "See you around, then," gave a laconic wave of his hand, and drove away.

"For small blessings, O Lord, make us truly grateful," she murmured, and Tillie smiled.

It was a quarter past seven and the rain clouds overhead were breaking apart into blobby gray and white puffs that chased the emerging sun across patches of bright blue sky.

The door knocker was a small cast-iron anchor, and Sigrid rapped it briskly.

"Coming, coming, coming!" caroled a cheerful voice through the open windows.

The cottage door flew open and Sue Montrose's freckle-faced smile of welcome turned into a look of blank surprise.

CHAPTER 22

Sue Montrose led them through the cottage to a tiny kitchen at the rear, where they found George Franklin barefoot in chinos and singing lustily as he whisked eggs in a stainless steel mixing bowl.

He turned at their entrance and his handsome face went from curiosity through total shock to sheepishness in rapid succession. Finally he managed a boyish smile, wiped his hands on the seat of his pants and held them both out to Sigrid.

"Did you bring your handcuffs, Lieutenant?"

"It was a possibility," Sigrid said coldly. "Did *you* forget we had an appointment, Mr. Franklin?"

"Not for one single second!" he assured her. "But my lawyer was tied up in court, Susie had disappeared, and you were acting like I'd killed her and Julie both, so I thought I'd better find her first."

"You seem to have done it very quickly," Sigrid observed.

"Well, I remembered that her uncle had this place—we were out here last fall—but I couldn't remember his name for the telephone listing or even the street, for that matter. It just seemed simpler to come. And I was right. Here she was."

He put his arm around Sue Montrose with a doting, slightly foolish grin.

Sigrid looked at Sue Montrose closely, sensing a new ease that hadn't been apparent Sunday afternoon. The tension between the couple had dissolved into a mushy honeymoon glow. She'd heard that love conquered all, but suspicion of murder, too?

"Perhaps now you won't mind answering our questions," she said.

Tillie accepted Sue Montrose's invitation to sit at the large round table, but Sigrid remained standing, her austere height giving her an unconscious psychological authority.

"Why was Julie Redmond blackmailing you?" she asked Franklin bluntly.

"Blackmail? What makes you think—"

"If we subpoena your bank records for the last three years," Sigrid interrupted, "do you deny that we'll find you paid her three hundred dollars every month for almost two years?"

"Now, Lieutenant, can you really do that?" he asked, smoothing down the thick dark curls that he'd carelessly mussed before. "You have to show cause or something, don't you? And I really don't think you can."

"Don't, George," said Sue Montrose, slipping away from his arm. She placed knives and forks in a pottery mug and set the mug on the table. "We're going to have to tell her about it sooner or later and it might as well be now. Get it over with."

She handed him the fork she'd been turning bacon with and faced Sigrid. "George explained everything to me last night," she said earnestly. "You're right—Julie had blackmailed him once."

"What for?"

Franklin muttered something, but Montrose laid her square little hand on his arm and he relaxed.

"Okay, Lieutenant," he said finally. "Remember Julie's dig about mistakes? I made a beaut a few years ago and if you think I'm going to give you all the details, forget it.

"Let's just say I had access to certain computer codes that tapped into a financial institution and I used them to borrow some money without anybody knowing. Except that I learned almost immediately that those codes were being set up to trap somebody else.

"Frankly, it scared the hell out of me. I replaced the funds instantly and covered my tracks completely."

"It was while Julie was still his secretary," said Sue. "She found a piece of incriminating evidence, but she didn't tell him at the time, just held onto it until she quit her job and didn't like living on what her husband gave her. George might not have been prosecuted but it would have made things awkward for him at Landau and Maas. Electronic security is their business, you know, and trust is a very important part of the image. So he paid her."

"And then last year you traded a tap on her telephone for the evidence she held?" asked Tillie, pleased to have one of his rare leaps in the dark proved correct.

"Seemed like an awful lot of trouble to go to for a divorce," said Franklin. "She said it was because of the new laws—that judges weren't giving out decent settlements anymore without hard proof. I guess she just wanted to clean him out good."

From the tone of his voice, Sigrid surmised that he didn't care what happened to Karl Redmond so long as he got out from under Julie's power. What could such a seemingly level-headed woman as Sue Montrose possibly see in this lazily amoral man? Granted he was as handsome as a daytime television actor, but did looks compensate for no character?

Evidently.

Sigrid decided against telling them what Julie Redmond had really wanted with the tap. Not that the death of a blameless old man would make any difference to Franklin, but she suspected that Montrose would view the knowledge differently and she didn't fancy herself as the apple-offering serpent in this seaside garden of Eden.

"For the record, where were you Saturday morning?" she asked Franklin.

Her question produced unexpected results. The man flushed a dark red and threw an anguished look at Sue Montrose, who dissolved in giggles.

"Dammit, Sue!"

"I'm sorry, darling."

But she didn't sound contrite, thought Sigrid, watching the girl lift sizzling strips of bacon from a red-enameled frying pan. Sue's lips twitched as Franklin picked up the bowl of eggs and began whisking them again with unnecessary violence.

She took the bowl from his hands and, like a mother prompting an unwilling child, said, "Tell the lieutenant where you were so we can get on with breakfast."

"I was at my hair stylist's," he said sulkily.

Sigrid was puzzled. "Hair stylist?"

"I go every week—shampoo, a trim, and—uh—styling."

Sigrid still didn't understand, but Tillie saw the point. "Hair weaving?" he asked shrewdly.

Franklin looked at them belligerently, daring them to laugh at him.

"I've got a receding hairline," he confided.

"All the way back to the top of his head," Sue added affectionately.

"So I supplement it a little," said Franklin. "For it to stay looking natural though, I have to keep it up. Every Saturday morning. I have a standing appointment."

"I thought he was seeing Julie then," said Sue. "He acted so secretive and guilty whenever I tried to get him to meet me on Saturday mornings."

"It's just not something a man likes to talk about," Franklin told them.

Especially not a man who prides himself on his virile appearance, thought Sigrid, as Tillie took down the salon's name and address. Well, if Montrose found his baldness endearing, more power to her.

The smell of bacon had filled the kitchen and reminded Tillie that he and the lieutenant had only had a doughnut apiece this morning.

"Won't you join us?" asked Sue Montrose, hospitable now that George's secrets were out in the open. "No trouble to throw some more bacon in the pan. Add a few eggs?"

Sigrid ignored Tillie's wistful face. "No, thank you,

Miss Montrose. We're almost finished and then we'll leave you to breakfast in peace. We'll still want you to sign the statement you gave me Sunday afternoon. Unless your discussion with Mr. Franklin last night has helped you remember something else since then?"

Sue missed the irony in the other woman's tone. "No, nothing," she answered innocently.

Nevertheless Sigrid asked her to recount once again her Saturday morning vigil, from the time Mrs. Cavatori rang Julie Redmond's bell at ten-fifteen until she herself entered at twelve-fifteen to find Julie cool to the touch.

Tillie looked at Sigrid curiously when she went back to that eleven-fifteen glass of milk.

"You say that someone from the Cavatori apartment went down on the elevator at eleven and again just before you left the door to get your milk. Are you sure that neither person crossed the vestibule to Redmond's apartment?"

"Positive."

"And you're equally positive that someone did in fact go down on that elevator at eleven-fourteen?"

"Where else would he go?" Sue Montrose asked sensibly. "I heard the door to 3-B open and close, the elevator came up, those doors opened and closed, then the elevator started back down. You can ask my uncles. One of them was on duty then, Uncle Sammy, I think."

"And then minutes after drinking your milk, you fell asleep?"

"A very light doze, Lieutenant, and only for a few minutes. I know I'd have heard if anybody'd come up then. That hall door is right beside the elevator shaft, if you recall."

Sigrid nodded, her mind suddenly so filled with speculations that she didn't realize what a stern gaze she had turned upon George Franklin.

The man cleared his throat uneasily and said, "Do I still have to bring my lawyer down and sign anything?"

Sigrid focused on him and brought herself back to the present. "I'm afraid so, Mr. Franklin. That tap might be an important element in another criminal investigation," she said, thinking of Mickey Novak.

"You mean she was blackmailing someone else?" asked Sue Montrose.

"Something like that."

"Oh God!" moaned Franklin.

"Your company may not have to learn of your involvement," Sigrid said, correctly interpreting his groan.

He brightened immediately. "Thanks, Lieutenant. You're a doll!"

The look she gave him with those slate gray eyes was so chilling that he was reminded that he had business in the refrigerator. Butter to find. Jam. A place to hide.

A mirthful Sue Montrose showed them out.

CHAPTER 23

With Tillie behind the wheel, they drove through Port Jefferson, looking for their turnoff back to New York. At least Tillie was looking. Sigrid was too preoccupied to pay more than mechanical interest to the streets they were passing.

He paused at a stop sign to allow a silver Volkswagen convertible on the through street to make a left turn past them, then proceeded leisurely on. In the rearview mirror, he noticed that the Volks had come to an abrupt halt and executed a hasty U-turn in the middle of the block.

As the little car zoomed up behind them, Tillie saw that the driver was a young woman with bright yellow hair. He edged over to give her room to pass, but she seemed content to follow. She followed much too closely for Tillie's liking and he speeded up.

She matched his speed.

Annoyed, he slowed again and thrust his arm out the window to wave her around.

"Something wrong?" Sigrid asked, finally noticing.

"Tailgater," he muttered.

Sigrid twisted around to look and when she did, the blonde waved and began blowing her horn.

"Hilda?" said Sigrid wonderingly.

"A friend of yours?"

"Cousin," she answered tersely. "Better pull over."

The Volkswagen convertible drew abreast of them and the driver broke into a delighted welcoming smile. "Siga! It *is* you! I don't believe it. What on earth are you doing in Port Jeff?"

"Actually, we were leaving it," Sigrid answered.

"*Leaving?* Without saying a word or stopping by for a cup of tea?" Even as she spoke, she was giving Tillie a thorough appraisal and Sigrid's heart dropped as she thought of the wild rumors that would soon be flying through the family if she left Hilda without fully allaying her suspicions.

From either side came impatient car horns as other vehicles tried to get around them in the narrow street.

"Follow me," said Hilda, and pulled ahead of them.

Tillie looked at Sigrid inquiringly.

Resigned, Sigrid nodded.

They were the same age and comparisons begun in childhood carried over to the present at rare family get-togethers. Hilda Sivertsen had been a plump and merry golden-haired child; as Hilda Carmichael, she was now a plump and merry young matron married to a CPA with a thriving business here on the Island. She also had a thriving family, as Tillie soon discovered.

"Hey, she has a baby with her!" he said, easing into the lane of traffic behind the open Volks. The padded infant seat beside her cousin had been strapped in so that the baby was riding backward, and only now had he noticed the tiny head bobbing inside.

Sigrid tried to recall the name of this last baby and found she couldn't even remember if it was a boy or a girl.

Fortunately, Hilda helped her out. As Sigrid performed the introductions in the driveway of Hilda's huge front yard—carefully stressing that Tillie was *Detective* Tildon and that they were in Port Jefferson on business—Hilda unstrapped the baby from its seat and said, "You haven't even met little Lars yet, Siga."

Then Sigrid remembered that the baby had been named for their mutual great-uncle, the closest thing she'd had to a grandfather in her father's family. She looked at the plump, tow-headed baby. His eyes were the exact same delft blue that Uncle Lars's eyes had been, and she suddenly felt very close to Hilda, who had loved the old man, too.

"I wish we could stay," she said and was surprised to realize that she meant it. "But we really are working."

"Then come back and visit soon," said Hilda. She had been a spontaneous, loving child and she gave Sigrid an impulsive hug. "We don't see you nearly often enough."

So seldom was she touched or caressed that Sigrid never knew how to respond. She always found herself going stiff and self-conscious, unable to return these casual shows of affection.

"She seems like a nice person," Tillie ventured, as they headed back to the city.

"She is," Sigrid said and turned the conversation back to more impersonal topics.

They stopped for a quick breakfast on their way in, and Tillie telephoned to arrange an interview with Karl Redmond while Sigrid ordered wheatcakes and sausage for them both.

"I didn't quite understand why you kept taking Montrose over that part about the milk," he said when his plate was nearly empty. "You think somebody could have come up on the elevator just as Vico Cavatori was going down?"

"No, that hadn't occurred to me," Sigrid said. She turned it over in her mind. "It is a possibility though. Think about it, Tillie: What if someone did arrive when Cavatori was leaving? If it's the murderer, he would quite logically wait a moment or two to see if anyone else was around. By the time he crossed the vestibule to the Redmond apartment, Sue Montrose would be in the kitchen, pouring milk."

"And when he left," said Tillie, "she would be dozing."

"So she wouldn't see him either time," Sigrid nodded.

"That's two coincidences, Lieutenant. I thought you didn't like coincidences."

"Just because I don't like them doesn't mean they never happen," Sigrid said wryly.

"Okay, but how did he leave? Not by the stairs. Novak's are the only footprints tracked through the fresh paint, and Montrose would have heard the elevator."

"Unless she was sleeping more soundly than she thought," said Sigrid. "I suppose the only sensible thing to do is ask Cavatori himself. Any word on how he's doing?"

"I called the hospital this morning after talking to you, and they said his condition had stabilized but he's still in the cardiac intensive care unit. That means nobody can see him except his immediate family."

"You'd better talk to the Dorritts again, then," she decided. "Try to pin Sammy down to the precise times that elevator went up and down Saturday morning."

She signaled for their check.

Most of the city's medallioned cabs are bright yellow, so Karl Redmond's assertion that he'd taken a yellow cab home Saturday morning wasn't much help.

"I'm sorry," he'd told Jim Lowry when that young police detective came to question him Sunday morning, "but I just didn't notice what fleet it was from."

"So then, of course, I asked him if he could describe the driver," said Jim Lowry.

It was Tuesday morning and he was sitting painfully on the edge of his hospital bed with his legs dangling as he spoke to Elaine Albee over the telephone.

"Are you sure you feel up to talking?" Elaine asked solicitously.

"I'm okay. They're letting me go home as soon as my doctor checks me out this morning."

It wasn't a subject he wanted to pursue. Especially not with her. A kneed groin wasn't like a bullet wound or a broken bone. It hurt like hell, but most people seemed to think it was funny. He'd listened closely but there was no hint of laughter lurking in Lainey's warm voice.

"So did Redmond remember the driver?" she asked, respecting his desire to keep the conversation all business.

"Yeah. It was a woman and her name was Carla. Carla with a C. He noticed that much because of his own name. No idea what the last name was, but you shouldn't have any trouble. Use the yellow pages on my desk; I checked off the ones I called, and I don't think there were many left."

There were seven, but Elaine got lucky on the second try.

"Yeah, we've got a Carla driving here," said the dispatcher at Silberman's Yellowbird Garage after the policewoman had identified herself. "Carla Berlinger. She'll be in at ten if you wanna talk to her."

The Yellowbird Garage was poorly lit and smelled of exhaust fumes and hot rubber. Elaine Albee sidestepped a puddle of grease just inside the wide doors and waited for her eyes to get used to the dimness before venturing across the wide expanse to the glassed-in office at the back. There she introduced herself to the motherly-looking dispatcher who pointed to a group of drivers at a table in the rear.

Carla Berlinger was a small, intense brunette in her early forties, dressed in jeans and a denim jacket. "My God, honey! What happened to you?" she exclaimed at the sight of Albee's colorful jaw.

"You should have seen it yesterday," Elaine said ruefully. "Someone kicked me."

"And I thought driving a hack was bad news!" Berlinger shook her head and led Elaine back to the front of the office. "I checked out my time sheets for Saturday morning," she said, "and that's all I know."

If Karl Redmond was vague about Carla Berlinger, her powers of observation weren't any better. "He must have been an average-looking Joe," she said. "Who can remember all those faces if there's nothing special about 'em?"

Still, they did have the time sheet and it confirmed Karl Redmond's story. Berlinger had picked up one male passenger at 11:03 Saturday morning on the corner of East Seventy-sixth Street and Third Avenue and dropped him off down in SoHo about twenty minutes later.

• • •

It was her day for babies and lovers, thought Sigrid, following Karl Redmond up the narrow stairs to the loft over Bryna Leighton's shop.

She had dropped Tillie at the office and, after a brief stop at a conventional jewelry store, had driven to SoHo.

Elaine Albee's report had been relayed to them when Tillie checked in via radio as they drove through Queens, so Sigrid no longer considered Redmond an active suspect; nevertheless, there was one small point she wanted to confirm herself.

Redmond had been waiting for her downstairs among the exotic costume jewelry, and her appearance surprised him. "Hey, you're the woman who was here with Bryna Saturday. I didn't know you were from the police." His thin face beamed at her. "Come on up and see the baby. You won't believe how much she's changed in three days!"

"I think it would be better—" Sigrid began, but Redmond was already halfway up the stairs and there was nothing to do but follow if she wanted to talk to him.

"She barely cries at all," Redmond confided. "You'd hardly know she was around."

Bryna Leighton sat nursing her infant daughter in a low rocking chair by the windows. With sunlight haloing her silver-blond hair, the baby's tiny pink hand upon her white breast, and the sweet smile of welcome on her lips, she looked more than ever like a Flemish Madonna.

"Sigrid!" she said softly. "How nice."

"Hello, Bryna," Sigrid said, suddenly feeling awkward again. She knew it was unprofessional to get personally involved during an investigation, but surely an exception could be made of little Katrina? She took a small gift-wrapped box from her purse and handed it to Bryna, who carefully removed the paper and lifted the lid.

It was a silver mug, chased with a garland of flowers around the lip and last Saturday's date engraved on the side.

"It's lovely," said Bryna. "Thank you. Want to hold her?"

"Oh no! I don't—I'm not used to—I wouldn't know how," she stammered; but before she knew what was happening, she found herself folded into Bryna's low rocker with the baby in her arms.

It was so incredibly tiny. Sigrid sat absolutely rigid, watching the diminutive mouth, abruptly deprived of milk, still make sucking movements. Surely it would start crying now.

Bryna laughed. "Relax, Sigrid. She's not going to break."

Cautiously, Sigrid let out the breath she'd been holding. There was a sweet smell of baby powder.

"Isn't she a marvel?" asked Karl Redmond. "Look at those long fingers!"

Sigrid looked. Long was a relative term, she decided. She'd seen dolls with longer fingers than that.

"And each fingernail so exquisitely made," crooned her father. "You forget between times how beautifully babies are made. Look at her little feet. And her ears! Did you ever see prettier ears?"

"Never." She said it so dryly that all three found themselves relaxing in warm laughter. Unprofessional or not, thought Sigrid, she liked them and that did make it harder to ask questions.

She handed the baby back to Bryna and said as much.

"It's okay," said Bryna. "We've nothing to hide, have we, Karl?"

He shook his head. "No one really thinks I could have killed Julie, do they?"

"Ex-husbands are always potential suspects," she said kindly, "but in your case, no. Not unless you bribed Mr. Cavatori, his maids, the doorman, and a cab driver to lie for you."

"You questioned every one of those people about me?"

"We did." She hesitated a moment, wondering if he'd ever suspected what a strong motive he had to kill his ex-wife.

"Has Timmy seen the baby?" she asked obliquely.

The boy's name sent a shadow across their faces.

"No," said Karl. "I went to visit him Sunday evening,

but he wouldn't even look at me. Just screamed if I tried to touch him. I remember when *he* was born—just like Katrina—so tiny . . ." His voice trailed off sadly. "He has his own lawyer now, did you know that? Vico said he needed someone objective to look after his interests. I guess that was in case I turned out to be Julie's murderer."

"Oh, Karl!" said Bryna, seeing the old hurt in his dear face. "Don't, love."

He smiled at her and gently lifted her free hand to his lips.

"It's okay. I guess it's best for Timmy if he stays with Vico and Luisa. They're crazy about him and he really loves them. They've been like his own grandparents ever since he was born. My father was killed last year, you know. Timmy probably doesn't even remember him."

"Then you haven't talked to Timmy's lawyer?" asked Sigrid.

"Hagstrom? No." He glanced at Bryna, but she shook her fair head, too.

Briefly, Sigrid described the opening of Julie's box at the bank yesterday—the money they'd found, the jewels and the tape.

Karl looked at her numbly. "She set Pop up?" he whispered. "She had Pop killed for some lousy diamonds?"

His face crumpled. "Oh God!" he sobbed. "Papa!"

Bryna thrust the baby back into Sigrid's startled grasp and instinctively gathered Karl into her arms.

CHAPTER 24

Sigrid felt tired when she drove back to headquarters and more than a little edgy. Karl and Bryna were nice people, she reflected. There was caring, respect, and mutual support, but emotional scenes always exhausted her and each visit to that SoHo loft had certainly been emotional.

It was a relief to return to the relative order of her office and she viewed Tillie's sensible, steady face with unaccustomed pleasure.

"Good news," he told her. "Mickey Novak's been picked up in Florence."

"*Florence?*" Sigrid was momentarily diverted. "Are we hooked into Interpol?"

"Not Florence, Italy." Tillie grinned. "Florence, South Carolina. He was apparently on his way to Florida. I've started the paperwork. We should get him back by the end of the week."

"Excellent," she said, thinking of Karl Redmond's anguish. At least one unsolved homicide would finally be closed. She rubbed the back of her neck and tried to concentrate on all the intertwined threads of this case. "Did you have a chance to question the Dorritts again?"

"I just came from there. Wait a second."

He flipped through his notebook until he came to the correct section. "Okay, here we are: Sammy Dorritt says he was in the lobby from eight-thirty till twelve noon on the dot. The only ones using the elevator around that time to go or come from the third floor were just as we thought—Karl Redmond came down around eleven and Vico Cavatori about ten or twelve minutes later. Neither of them went back up.

"The other tenants who used the elevator during that particular period were an elderly couple from the fourth floor and a baby-sitter and two children from the seventh. I think we can eliminate them?"

Sigrid agreed. "So much for our double coincidence murderer," she said glumly.

"You wouldn't have liked it anyhow," Tillie consoled her absentmindedly, looking back through his notes.

Sigrid looked at him suspiciously, but he really was absorbed in his notebook.

It had been the sort of remark and in the same tone of voice Nauman might have used. She gave herself a brief moment to think of Nauman; to remember how he liked to needle her. She wondered how long he'd be tied up in Amsterdam and if the museum's staff included any cute young things or if—oh, hell!

"Did you say something, Lieutenant?"

"Never mind, Tillie. Let me see your timetable again. We must be missing something obvious."

She studied his figures with a growing sense of frustration. It seemed improbable that Mickey Novak had killed his sister, however neat a solution that would make. True, he was a self-confessed thief and murderer, condemned by his own taped voice; but the necklace had been ripped from Julie Redmond's neck *after* she was dead and Sue Montrose was positive that her body had been cool to the touch minutes after Novak first entered the apartment.

Sammy Dorritt said Vico Cavatori had emerged from the elevator at the time he said and Montrose hadn't seen him cross her line of sight. Ditto for Karl Redmond. Vico had ushered him into the elevator; Dorritt had seen him

leave it and exit from the building. Elaine Albee had efficiently located the cab driver who had picked him up
almost immediately afterward.

Sue Montrose had seen no one else enter or leave the
apartment except Luisa Cavatori and Timmy Redmond
and Julie had been alive then, had called instructions to
Timmy to be good.

Poor Timmy. As if he could be naughty, as cowed as
he'd probably been by his mother. He was still young
enough that he might not suffer permanent emotional scars
from the brusque treatment she'd given him. Luisa and
Vico Cavatori had provided stable love all along and under
their guardianship, that stability would continue.

Unless—

There was that unbidden thought again which Dorritt's
statement couldn't completely erase, but she really didn't
want to face all the emotional ramifications such a theory
conjured up. Not now. She'd had enough of emotions for
one day.

She rubbed the back of her neck again and looked at the
clock. It was only three-fifteen, but she told Tillie, "Let's
call it a day."

Instead of going straight home, Sigrid found herself
drawn to the health spa where she was a member. In the
locker room she stripped and changed into a one-piece
white swim suit, mechanically piled her long hair on top
of her head, tucked it into a white bathing cap, and headed
out to the Olympic-sized pool.

Since childhood, swimming had been a solace for her.
If she had been asked to analyze her feelings about the
water, she would have said that swimming was good exercise, a means of unwinding physically, nothing more.

But so intense was her need today that she was almost
running when she entered the large tiled space, felt the
warm moist air and smelled again the flat aroma of chlorine.
Everything here was clean, uncluttered, unadorned and
utterly satisfying in its Spartan rigor. Flat white planes,
sharp angles, only the water itself soft and flowing.

The pool was divided into marked lanes for serious swimmers and an unmarked area for general puddlers. There was only one other girl in the lanes and she was concentrating on wind sprints. Sigrid chose an empty lane farthest from her and dived in.

Her mind went blank as she stroked her way through the water, one arm over the other in steady synchronization. She did three quick laps, then turned over and backstroked at a more leisurely pace.

The water lifted her up and she moved through it almost effortlessly after that first furious spurt. The water slid along her boy-slim body, pulling her out of herself, as her arms stretched wide. In the water, she could reach out and give herself up to an unacknowledged sensuousness that would be unthinkable with people.

Nauman's image floated in her mind and she didn't fight it. Here in the water, she felt no responsibility for undisciplined thoughts that would have been banished at another time and place.

Nauman's face soon drifted into Karl Redmond's. She watched again while Karl clung to Bryna with great sobs wracking his body until at last Bryna took their infant daughter from Sigrid and made Karl hold her.

She thought of Hilda's baby Lars and of Great-uncle Lars, who had taken them to Prospect Park as children and bought them peanuts to feed the pigeons and who had seemed to know that even though Sigrid couldn't emulate Hilda's prodigal hugs and kisses, her stiff little body held a love just as fiercely given. Uncle Lars had been dead nine years and she still missed his uncritical acceptance, the way his blue eyes lit up whenever she appeared.

As the emotional tensions which had been building up in her all day were sluiced away in the limpid, translucent water, Sigrid relaxed enough to think consciously of more mundane issues. Her apartment, for instance.

Roman Tramegra had called it mediocre and she supposed it was by some standards. It was a straightforward utilitarian set of rooms, adequate space and comfortable enough, but he was right—there was nothing to differentiate it from thousands of other similar apartments throughout the city. No particular charm to it; nevertheless, it had been a fixed fact of life these last few years and she didn't want to move.

Yet here in the water, she could even consider it. Could contemplate the disorder and upheaval without last night's dismay.

She touched the tiled edge of the pool, flipped onto her stomach, and began a final series of serious laps.

CHAPTER 25

As she headed home, completely refreshed now, a name suddenly floated up from Sigrid's subconscious: Gilbert Fitzpatrick. They had forgotten all about that prim and fussy little lawyer whom Julie Redmond had delighted in tormenting.

She unlocked the door to her apartment and hurried in so quickly that she almost collided with Roman Tramegra advancing to open the door for her.

"My dear Sigrid," he boomed. "How *wonderful* that you're home early. I—"

"Excuse me a minute, Roman," she said, and made for the telephone. A child's voice answered and said, "Daddy's not here. He's helping Chuckie play ball."

"What about your mother?"

"Mommy's here." Sigrid heard a clunk as the phone at the other end hit the table. A distant infantile voice called, "Mommy!" In the background came the painful strains of someone practicing scales on the violin. Someone very new at it.

"Hello?" said Marian Tildon's unruffled voice.

Sigrid identified herself and asked if Tillie could call her at home when he'd finished playing ball. Marian cheerfully agreed to relay the message.

"Sigrid, my dear," said Roman when she had hung up, "I must tell you something—that is, *ask* you something—*most* important."

"Very well," she said and waited expectantly.

But things were seldom that simple with Roman. She had to be seated comfortably on the couch; had to assure him that, no, she did not wish to change clothes first, she still felt fresh from her swim; and yes, she had time to listen.

Tramegra smoothed his sandy hair carefully over his bald spot and Sigrid's heart sank. Nervous apprehension was not a trait she'd seen in him so far. He had never discussed the personal problems which had sent him fleeing home from Europe and she hoped this didn't signal the opening of emotional floodgates.

"Is the sun over the yardarm yet?" he asked finally. "I brought sherry. Such a *civilized* drink, don't you think? Highballs and cocktails have their place, of course, but conversation is so often impeded after two or three glasses. Whereas with sherry . . ."

As he fetched and poured and gave her a capsulated history of the difference between amontillado and manzanilla, Sigrid suddenly realized that something about the room was different. He had shifted some of the furniture closer together and over by the window, afternoon sunlight was caught by green glass cat eyes.

"You've finished the chair!" she said. "Why, Roman, it's magnificent."

She was not being polite. Freed of that ugly brown paint, the mellow wood glowed with subtle tones, and the seat and tall back had been reupholstered with surprising skill and taste. She had originally envisioned some fabric in perhaps moss green, but he had found a material of predominately dark red tones that reminded her of a medieval tapestry.

"Do you really like it?" asked Tramegra. "I know you said plain fabric, but really, my dear, you were made for elegance. Go ahead, *do* try it out."

Sigrid crossed the room with her glass of sherry and sat

down. It truly was a regal chair. A chair of state. A chair in which to receive ambassadors. She lifted her glass to his accomplishment.

"Perfect!" crowed Tramegra. "All you need now is a polished oak refectory table."

"A refectory table?" The image appealed to her. "But there's no space here for a table that big. Besides, most of my things are modern and it wouldn't fit it."

"Nonsense! Eclecticism is in. I sold an article on it to *Urban House* only last year. And as for more space, it's odd you should mention it, for that's what I wanted to discuss. You see—"

The telephone rang. "Sorry," Sigrid apologized.

As expected, it was Tillie. "Marian said you wanted me to call, Lieutenant?"

"That's right. Listen, Tillie, did we ever confirm Gilbert Fitzpatrick's alibi?"

There was a silence. "Tillie?"

"Just a minute, Lieutenant, I'm checking my notes. Fitz-patrick, Eliza . . . Elizabeth . . . Gilbert. Here we are. Okay, Jim Lowry interviewed a Taylor Breedlove, who stated that he and Gilbert Fitzpatrick played squash last Saturday morning from ten till twelve at a gym near West Twenty-third Street. Sorry."

"It was just a thought," sighed Sigrid.

"Anyhow," Tillie pointed out, "how could he have gotten past Montrose? Your coincidences, again?" His tone was lightly teasing.

"Don't be impertinent," she said, but she didn't really mean it. Light banter wasn't their usual style; Tillie must have had a relaxing, buoying afternoon, too, she thought. "One last thing—do you have Mr. Cavatori's hospital number there?"

He did and she copied it onto the pad by her telephone. "Thanks, Tillie."

"No bother. See you tomorrow, Lieutenant."

She turned back to Tramegra and found him refilling her glass. "I'm sorry, Roman, what were you saying about more space?"

He swallowed his sherry and blurted, "My dear, you

must give me haven. I've nowhere else to turn and I simply can *not* remain in your mother's apartment another night. It's that Stewart woman.

"My dear, she has *no* shame! She thinks I'm a guide to American culture. She actually wanted me to let them watch me take a shower so they could get the hang of it; and when I refused, *she* did it herself! Mother-naked, without the curtain. Water three inches deep on the floor.

"I *approve* of the melting pot, truly I do. I *know* we are all immigrants—except for the Indians . . . American Indians, of course, not East or West Indians—but I'm starting to feel like boiled cabbage.

"Heaven surely knows they mean well. They nod and bow and smile, but they watch *every* move I make! And they're so incredibly *tiny*. I keep expecting to step on one of them accidentally. My dear, *think* how you'd feel if you stepped on someone's grandmother."

"But, Roman, where can I put you?" Sigrid said helplessly. "You can't sleep on the couch. I mean—"

"My dear, I understand. You don't wish your privacy invaded any more than I. But it's only until I find suitable quarters. And I *promise* you," he said in his earnest bass profundo, "you'll hardly know I'm here. Now that the chair is finished, I can tuck a cot into that little workroom. I won't come out until you've left for work and I'll go in *immediately* after dinner. Dear Sigrid, please say yes."

"Well—"

"Ah, *bless* you, child! You won't regret it."

Sigrid was dubious. She lived alone by definite choice and thought she'd left the complications of roommates behind at college long years ago. Evidently there was to be a reprise.

"After all, you don't plan to be here very long yourself," Roman reminded her.

"Oh damn! That's right." Those co-op plans, she thought. Her lease expired in August.

"Not to worry," he said. "While I look for my own place, I shall keep an eye out for you. Indeed, I shall repay your hospitality by finding you a new and much better apartment."

"Would you really?" she asked incredulously, since the worst thing about moving was first finding a new place.

"My pleasure. Where would you like to live?"

"Somewhere within walking distance of work would be nice. Or around Greenwich Village?"

He nodded. "And how much are you willing to pay?"

Sigrid made a quick mental survey of her monthly expenses and gave a figure.

Tramegra's eyes widened slightly. "I had *no* idea that the city paid its police officers that well."

"I've been moonlighting," she said in an unaccustomed flight of fancy. Tramegra looked startled and she gave herself a mental shake. She seemed to be irresponsibly giddy this afternoon. Was it the sherry? She set the glass down and said, "No, it's just that I've been on the force a long time. Seniority starts to mean something after ten years."

Tramegra drained his own glass and stood up purposefully. "I've already packed, so I'll just go and pick up my things and be back within the hour."

When he'd gone, Sigrid rose and fixed herself a stiff gin and tonic before surveying the logistics of her apartment. The master bath could only be reached by going through her bedroom, but there was a tiny half-bath off the hall. She hoped Roman wasn't a devotee of long, soaking baths. She brought soap and extra towels and sorted through her linens for sheets and a blanket. If Roman didn't have his own pillow, he could use one of the little cushions from the couch.

Odd how things came full circle, she mused. She'd hated her mother's frequent moves and here she was faced with one herself. Again, throughout her childhood after her father died, their spare beds and couches had overflowed with a succession of sleepovers—Anne's friends and relatives, just passing through, temporarily jobless or simply waiting out a domestic crisis—yet Roman was the first overnight guest of her own.

She hoped she wasn't setting a precedent. She liked her mother, but she really didn't want to follow in Anne's footsteps.

By the time Roman returned, Sigrid had forestalled one

of his inedible concoctions by opening a can of tomato soup, grilling some cheese sandwiches and shredding the remains of a head of lettuce that had turned brown around the edges.

"This is the last supper you'll have to cook for the next three months," he promised, and shooed her out of the kitchen after they'd eaten.

Sigrid picked up the folder she'd brought home from work and pulled a table over to her new chair. Roman was right. A refectory table would be perfect for spreading out her papers. Maybe in the new apartment.

She tried to concentrate on the data before her, a summarization of other matters for Captain McKinnon; but her mind kept wandering back to Julie Redmond's murder. There was no avoiding it.

While Roman clattered pots and pans in the kitchen sink, Sigrid dialed the number Tillie had given her.

"Cardiac Intensive Care Family Waiting Room, Mrs. Bazemore speaking."

Sigrid identified herself and asked about Mr. Cavatori.

"He's doing splendidly," said Mrs. Bazemore. "Much stronger than they thought. In fact, he was moved into a private room on the seventh floor late this afternoon. One moment, Lieutenant, and I'll see if I can switch you."

There were clickings and rings, then a crisper voice said, "Mr. Cavatori's room; Miss Levanthal here."

Again Sigrid stated her name and added, "New York Police Department."

"I'm Mr. Cavatori's nurse. He's resting now, Lieutenant Harald, and cannot possibly speak over the telephone yet."

"What about visitors?" Sigrid asked, putting equal crispness into her own voice.

"I suppose if it were official, something could be arranged," the nurse said disapprovingly. "Tomorrow would be better though."

"Is Mrs. Cavatori there?"

"No, she left about five minutes ago to go home for some of Mr. Cavatori's things. I expect her back around nine."

"Very well," said Sigrid. She hung up thoughtfully,

feeling a little melancholy as she thought of Vico Cavatori's fragile health. How sad it must be for Luisa Cavatori to go back to an empty apartment.

Not literally empty, of course. Not with Timmy and the two maids there, but without Cavatori? They seemed so devoted. Like Baucis and Philemon.

She wondered what it would be like to love someone that deeply and to know how precariously that person's life is balanced. Unbidden, a fleeting memory of Nauman's vigorous health spun itself across her conscious mind, but this time she brushed it away.

There's no point in getting sentimental or maudlin about it, she told herself, but perhaps everything worked out for the best after all. There were worse ways to die than by a heart attack, and Timmy Redmond might give Mrs. Cavatori a continuing focus for all that overflowing maternalism.

Children were said to be a comfort.

Sigrid stood up, stretched and went into her bathroom where she splashed water on her face, unloosed the neat bun at the nape of her neck and brushed out the long dark hair.

She started to change clothes, had already unbuttoned her shirt, when, from the other part of the apartment, she heard the deep rumble of Roman Tramegra's solemn voice. She rebuttoned her shirt, stepped into the hall, and listened. Had someone come? She strained to hear the other person, but since the kitchen door was closed, all that reached her were the tones and cadences of Tramegra's conversation as he spoke, paused for reply, then spoke again.

Sigrid pushed open the kitchen door and found Roman alone except for the caterpillars on the parsley and the mayonnaise jar that still held the Io larva he'd bought the night before. He had set up his camera and tripod and was constructing a backdrop of twigs upon her kitchen counter.

"I thought for a moment that someone had come," Sigrid said.

"Oh no, my dear, just me talking to the little blighters. I say, have a look and tell me how many of the swallowtails you find."

Sigrid obliged. "I only see two—no, wait a minute. There's a third."

"Actually, there are four of them, you know," said Tramegra, taking a reading with his light meter. "Amazing how they blend into their background. Right under your eyes and you don't see them."

"It *is* amazing," said Sigrid slowly. She stood transfixed, comparing the scene in her kitchen with the way it must have happened in the Rensselaer Building last Saturday morning.

Leaving Roman with his caterpillar herd, she wandered back to the telephone and called Sue Montrose, who was still out in Port Jefferson.

The questions she asked were clear and to the point, and when she hung up, Sigrid thought she knew how Julie Redmond had been killed. The why was still a muddle. Unless it was for the same motive that had been dogging her thoughts for the last two days . . .

"Would you like an espresso before I begin shooting?" Roman called.

"No, thank you," she answered. "I'm afraid I have to go out again."

CHAPTER 26

Sigrid pressed her back against the service door to apartment 3-A of the Rensselaer Building and looked around the vestibule for a long moment before crossing in front of the elevator to ring the bell at 3-B.

Luisa Cavatori opened the door with a burst of Italian which died as she recognized Sigrid.

"*Mi scusa,* Lieutenant. I thought you were Giuseppina. Always she forgets her key. Come in! Come in! If only for a few minutes. I must go back to the hospital soon. You know about my Vico?"

Sigrid nodded. "I was very sorry to hear," she said.

"Again, we are lucky though," the woman beamed. "Already he is better. God is merciful after all. Sit here," she invited, patting the couch beside her. "Would you like a glass of wine, Lieutenant? More I cannot offer, since Maria is out also."

"No, nothing," Sigrid said.

"Then how may I help you?" asked Luisa Cavatori. "Tell me."

It was an intensely awkward moment for Sigrid, and she

gazed across the room to the candle that seemed to burn perpetually on the carved sideboard.

"I have a friend," she said. "He talks to caterpillars."

"I am sorry, Lieutenant Harald, I do not understand."

"Neither did I for a long time. Not until I heard the caterpillars not talking back just now." She kept her wide gray eyes on the candle. "Until then I wondered if Mr. Cavatori had killed Julie Redmond. Of everyone, he seemed to have had the most opportunity."

"My Vico? A bug he could kill, maybe even a mouse, but a person? Julie? Never!"

"No," Sigrid said quietly, "but you could. I'm not sure why you did it, though. Will you tell me?"

Sigrid held her breath and silence grew in the room until it blocked out even the muffled sounds of traffic from the street below.

When Luisa Cavatori didn't speak, Sigrid risked a look at her face and was shocked. It was if a plump, juicy apple had suddenly turned into a withered fig—the vitality and lively animation that had flashed in those gleaming eyes and bloomed in her translucent complexion had drained away. For the first time, Luisa Cavatori looked her full age.

In the semi-twilight, her voice when at last she spoke was soft and contemplative.

"Life! It's enough to make a stone man laugh. The things you want so bad and never get. You get what someone else wants and they have what you would sell your soul for, no?"

Sigrid didn't answer, but Mrs. Cavatori didn't seem to expect her to.

"We were very poor, Vico and me; and when we came to America, there was money to be made if you worked hard enough. And Vico, how he worked! I'll make you a contessa, he said, and everything he has given me. Everything!

"Except a child.

"At first we were too poor and then came the war. Our family in *Italia*—Vico and I are cousins, you know?—they had so little. We had so much. Could we forget our own, let them starve? We were still young. Next year, we said; little by little all things come.

"But when next year finally came, it was too late. No babies could we make.

"Everywhere I went, to all the expensive doctors and all, *all* said, '*Mi dispiaccio, signora.* There is nothing we can do.'

"So finally we say, all right, it's God's will; and we write to Vico's brother who is poor in money but rich in children and we say, you have so many; give us please one child to love and make our son.

"That is how Paolo came to us."

Her eyes sought one of the silver-framed photographs illuminated by the votive candle across the darkening room.

"He was ten when he came. A baby he was not, but he was of our blood and so *gioioso*—so laughing—after the long childhood of war.

"For six years we had a son and such a son he was! Today mothers see their children have a needle or eat a little cube of sugar and what's to worry? But in 1952, who ever heard of Jonas Salk or Doctor Sabin? Iron lungs could not breathe strong enough for our Paolo."

Mrs. Cavatori sighed and stood heavily to switch on a lamp and draw the curtains across the afterglow which lingered over the city. With her back to the heavy scarlet drapes, she examined the police officer matter-of-factly and Sigrid could see the brisk vitality return to her face.

"You listen much too good, young woman"—she smiled shrewdly—"but if you expect me to weep on your shoulder and say yes, I murdered Julie because she had a child and I have not; because she abused the child and I wanted to give him love—"

She shrugged contemptuously. "You waste your time. And mine. I must dress now and go back to the hospital. My Vico will want me."

"But you *did* kill her, didn't you?" Sigrid persisted.

"If you think so, prove it."

"I can't, except circumstantially," Sigrid admitted.

A flick of Luisa Cayatori's fingers showed how little she feared the flimsy case woven around her.

"But there's motive," Sigrid said thoughtfully, "and certainly there was opportunity. You went to take the boy to the circus and something had happened. He'd spilled cereal on his pants and had been sent to his room. Julie Redmond seems to have been a self-centered, short-tempered woman who lashed out at whoever was closest when she was angry.

"Maybe she said Timmy couldn't go to the circus and when you tried to argue, perhaps she lost her temper with you? Yes, of course! You're the one Miss Fitzpatrick heard her arguing with, weren't you? The one at whom she screamed, 'He's mine!'

"She wasn't going to let you have Timmy anymore, was she?"

"She would have broken Vico's heart. And Timmy's." Luisa Cavatori's eyes glittered dangerously and her voice deepened with primitive emotion. "She was jealous of how Timmy loved us."

"You kept your voice down," said Sigrid, "but not your temper. When she threatened to keep Timmy from you permanently, you picked up that flatiron and smashed her with it."

"Then she got up and told Timmy goodbye when we left?" parried Mrs. Cavatori scornfully.

"Did she? You called to her from the front hall as you left and you prompted him to say goodbye, too; but did she really answer or was that something you planted in a baby's mind?"

"And what did *she* do to his mind?" demanded Mrs. Cavatori. Her voice smoldered with intense anger. "Always picking on him, yelling, hitting. Nothing could he do to please her. A dog in the hay she was, hating the child and hating his father and teaching him to fear. You know Pavlov? Of course. Conditioned reflex. Big words, but easy to do. So easy. Every time Karl took Timmy out, when Timmy came home, she would slap him and jeer at him and put him through torment!

"No wonder Timmy ran and hid and cried when his papa came. No matter how nice Karl tried to be one day a week, it was Julie that Timmy had to live with the other six days."

"That's motive enough," Sigrid said. "With Timmy afraid of Redmond and Redmond's resignation to the situation, wanting only for his son to be happy, you knew you stood a good chance to get Timmy for yourself.

"And that business contract your husband arranged with Karl Redmond—was that business or a bribe? Was he buying a product or a child? Did you plan to adopt Timmy legally?"

"I thought of it," Luisa Cavatori answered calmly. "All Saturday afternoon, I thought of it; but I am a superstitious old woman. Twice God has shown me that Vico and I were not meant to have children. I would not risk Timmy to tempt Him a third time.

"Julie Redmond was a bad woman and a worse mother and I am not sorry she is dead, *ma guarda!*—I do not say I killed her. And I have no profit by her death."

She gestured toward the hall which led to the bedrooms. "You think Timmy is here? No. Karl came for him an hour ago. It is not easy to uncondition a child. He was still afraid when they left, *but!* he was not crying.

"All these days I did give nice thoughts to him for his father and for his new little sister. Karl Redmond is a kind man and perhaps that woman is good also. She wanted Karl to bring Timmy to their home before now. Little by little, when Timmy sees the sky does not fall in on him, he will be easy and learn to love. A boy should be with his own. He will be happy.

"So! Where now is your circumstance and motive? Say quickly, for I must go to Vico."

"It's not for me to say," Sigrid answered slowly. "I'll turn my findings over to the District Attorney's office. They'll decide."

Mrs. Cavatori tossed her head. "I think, Lieutenant Harald, they will decide you have no case."

A cold anger began to build inside Sigrid as she realized how very little hard evidence there was upon which to base a strong prosecution. Sue Montrose would testify that she had not heard Julie's voice that morning and the medical evidence would argue that Julie had been killed during the period Mrs. Cavatori was there, but neither would be enough.

She remembered how she'd felt at seeing Julie Redmond dead on the floor of her yellow and orange kitchen. A spoiled and amoral woman, she knew now. An unfit mother. A woman who blackmailed her ex-lover, helped arrange her father-in-law's murder, and cheated her own brother.

But Luisa Cavatori hadn't known all that last Saturday morning.

"Maybe you've almost rationalized it and decided she deserved to die for blighting the child," said Sigrid, "but I don't think any of those noble thoughts were in your mind when you picked up that flatiron. I think you smashed her just because she tried to thwart you and keep you from having your own way with Timmy."

Mrs. Cavatori shrugged indifferently, impatient for Sigrid to be gone.

Sigrid looked across the room to the crucifix and photographs beside the bowl of anemones and she thought of the yellow roses that had sat on Julie Redmond's white desk.

Nothing was neat and tidy in this world, things were seldom what they should be and justice often miscarried; but to acquiesce in private executions was to open the door to everything that she abhorred by nature and by training.

And then she remembered Vico Cavatori's wise face and the old man's radiant goodness. Luisa Cavatori might not stand trial, might never spend a single day in jail, but there were other punishments.

The older woman read it in her eyes as Sigrid turned from her and headed for the door.

"You can*not!*" she cried. "I won't let you! It will kill him. Besides, my Vico will never believe you! He *won't!*"

"He'll believe," Sigrid said coldly. "He'll believe because he won't ask me. He'll ask you."

She paused in the doorway and stared implacably at the white-faced woman. "Can you lie to him?"

Luisa Cavatori stared back bleakly without speaking. Sigrid nodded and closed the door silently behind her.

MARGARET MARON
lives with her artist husband on their family
farm near Raleigh, North Carolina. She is a
former president of Sisters in Crime.